This book is to be returned on or before
the last date stamped below.

Other books by Karen McCombie

The *Ally's World* series

A Guided Tour of Ally's World
My V. Groovy Ally's World Journal

The *Stella Etc.* series

Marshmallow Magic and the Wild Rose Rouge
An Urgent Message of Wowness
My Funny Valentine
Wonderland

**To find out more about Karen McCombie,
visit her website www.karenmccombie.com**

KAREN McCOMBIE

Bliss...

■SCHOLASTIC

Scholastic Children's Books
An imprint of Scholastic Ltd
Euston House, 24 Eversholt Street
London, NW1 1DB, UK
Registered office: Westfield Road, Southam, Warwickshire, CV47 0RA
SCHOLASTIC and associated logos are trademarks and or registered
trademarks of Scholastic Inc.

First published in the UK by Scholastic Ltd, 2002
This edition published by Scholastic Ltd, 2007

10 digit ISBN 1 407 10299 0
13 digit ISBN 978 1 407 10299 3

British Library Cataloguing-in-Publication Data
A CIP catalogue record for this book is available from the British Library

Printed in the UK by CPI Bookmarque, Croydon, CR0 4TD
Papers used by Scholastic Children's Books are made from wood
grown in sustainable forests.

1 3 5 7 9 10 8 6 4 2

www.scholastic.co.uk/zone

*For Marina, who started the
whole ball rolling. . .*

chapter one
Cosmic clues (oh yeah?)

Date: *Wednesday 12th June*

Frame of mind: *Nauseous*

Twists of Fate: *Knots in my stomach, more like.*

"'VIRGO: 24 August–23 September.

Whay-hey! Here comes summer, and if you want an indication of what the next few months of sunshine have in store for you, then look no further than this week for cosmic clues. Oh, yes – it's time to set your Virgoan radar on tracking and pick up what Fate's got planned!

Lucky Day: Thursday 13 June.'"

"That's mine, is it?" I ask, after Jude stops reading aloud from the horoscope page of her magazine.

To be honest, I was only half-listening – I guess I'm sort of *mildly* interested in stars and stuff, but I usually forget what they said five minutes after I've read them. Anyway, I'm slightly distracted by the large pile of maths books scattered on my bedroom floor, staring up at me. Somehow, I have to shoehorn all that information into the maths-free zone that's my head today, if I've got any chance of passing the exam tomorrow.

"Excuse me, you *are* the only Virgoan in the room, right? Were you too busy with some illustrious thought to be paying attention, Ms Palmer?" Shaunna eyeballs me, sticking her hands on her hips and doing an uncanny impersonation of Mrs Klein, our demon maths teacher.

"Yes, I *am* the only Virgoan, and yes, I *was* paying attention – kind of. I just never know what horoscopes are trying to *say*. Why can't they be written in plain English? It's like they're some weird, complicated code that I can't figure out."

"Like algebra equations?" Jude suggests.

"Don't remind me. . ."

I flop face-first into my squashy duvet, glad of

2

the sudden dark blotting out my irritatingly relaxed friends and the ominous pile of books I haven't a hope in hell of understanding.

I know, I know, I *know* I should have started swotting earlier, but I've been kind of . . . distracted lately.

"What's up with you? You've gone really gloomy on us recently, Molly!"

Gloomy – is that how Shaunna sees me? I'm usually the practical one out of the three of us. That's how it works: Shaunna's the funny one, I'm the sensible one, and Jude . . . well, Jude's just a bit scatty – worrying and daydreaming a speciality. Except she's not the one doing the worrying just now; it's me.

"She's allergic to exams," I hear Jude explain to Shaunna.

That's true. It's like these stupid exams have been going on for ever, sucking all the joy out of my life. But that's not *all* that's doing my head in.

"Only one more to go, Mol, and then you'd better start getting happy again!"

Easy for Shaunna to say – she's not living inside my head, which lately has been just a mush of German verbs, examples of allegories, chunks of the Russian Revolution, and thoughts of. . .

"Dean coming round today?"

"No," I mumble a reply to Jude straight into my duvet.

Dean.

If Dean had a fan club, it'd have Shaunna, Jude and my entire family as die-hard members. Dean is the text-book perfect boyfriend: "*Shaunna*'s dated him, *you*'ve been going out with him for ever, Molly – so when do *I* get a turn?" Jude once joked. The answer is she doesn't (get a turn, I mean) – Dean's mine, all mine.

But you know something? Right now, I kind of wish Shaunna and Jude didn't like him *quite* so much. Then maybe I'd be able to talk to them about all the mad thoughts running around in my head, without them telling me I'm being stupid, or worse still, thinking badly of Dean, when he hasn't done anything wrong. But then maybe it's nothing to do with them . . . it's between me and Dean, right? Right? Except I don't really know how to say anything to him either. How do I start? "Hey, Dean, about that night a couple of weeks ago. . ."

"Well, if you're not going to be any fun, we're going!" Shaunna calls out. "See you tomorrow at the exam hall!"

"Bye, Molly. Here – I'm finished with this. You can have it if you want. . ."

There's a rustle of paper and air and a thump, as Jude chucks the magazine and it lands somewhere beside my ear.

"Thanks, bye. . ." I mumble, wiggling my hand limply as they pad out of my room.

After I hear the front door bang, I reluctantly prop myself up on my elbows and let my gaze fall on the opened page of the magazine (well, anything to avoid facing those looming textbooks).

. . .if you want an indication of what the next few months of sunshine have in store for you, then look no further than this week for cosmic clues. . .

Call me cynical, but what's that supposed to mean, exactly? And anyway, I know what the next few months of sunshine have in store for me – complete boredom, since I'm the only person I know that hasn't sorted themselves out with a summer job (not for the lack of trying).

Lucky Day: Thursday 13 June.

Uh . . . I don't *think* so. That's tomorrow, and that's the worst exam of the lot.

It's dumb, it doesn't make sense, and it's probably made up. So how come I find myself reading my horoscope again, and again, and again?

Maybe it's because right now, all my sensible thinking and analysing and common sense isn't helping to sort out the mush in my head one little bit. Maybe it would be a relief – fun, even – if I stopped being this typical, rational Virgo my horoscopes always tell me I am and hand over responsibility to fate. Maybe I should do what this says and keep an eye out for those cosmic clues that are meant to be magically popping up all over the place, telling me what I should (or shouldn't?) be doing.

Or maybe I just need to drag myself off this bed and start revising. Yeah, I'll get started on that straight away, right after I lie here for a while longer and think about me and Dean and . . . everything.

Guess I'll be kissing that maths exam goodbye. . .

chapter two

Hello trees, hello sky...

Date: *Thursday 13th June*

Frame of mind: *Blissed out*

Twists of Fate: *So many it's silly...*

"Is your face broken?" Shaunna grins, suddenly looming over me, her head of long, wavy brown hair blocking out the early summer sunlight.

Me, Shaunna and Jude have been lying here on our backs on the daisy-splattered lawns of Westburn Park for the last half an hour, getting grass stains on our school uniform (but not caring), with our heads practically touching and our bare feet (school shoes kicked off) radiating outwards and forming all three points of some mystical, invisible triangle.

At least that's what I said to Shaunna and Jude five minutes ago, but they just laughed at me. Not that I mind. And I don't mind that Shaunna seems to be teasing me again now.

"What are you on about?" I blink up at her.

"I'm on about that stupid smile of yours, Molly Palmer – it's still there. You've had that stuck on your face since first thing this morning; since before we even went into the exam room."

It's true. There were plenty of people smiling nervous smiles of relief at the *end* of our maths exam (specially since it was the last day of exams and first day of freedom), but I must have been the only person grinning going *into* the exam hall in the first place.

"I thought you *wanted* me to cheer up!"

"Molly, I wanted you to get *happy*," says Shaunna, "not turn all freaky on us. . ."

I know they think it's kind of *fruitcake*, all the stuff I've just told them about: the coincidences that have happened around me today; the way Fate seemed to be letting me in on some cosmic secret (that I don't quite understand yet), *just* like my horoscope said. But I shrug and close my eyes, happy to be a freak if it means my personal little cloud of gloom seems to have finally floated off somewhere.

"You're going to have to watch yourself now, Molly." Jude widens her dark eyes, as she rolls over on to her elbows like Shaunna and stares down at me.

"And why am I going to have to watch myself?" I ask an upside-down, spiky-haired Jude, still smiling the smile I can't seem to wipe off my face.

"'Cause with all this spook stuff you've been spouting today, people might want to burn you as a witch!"

"Oh, ha, ha, ha," I reply dryly, rolling my eyes at Jude, which must look really bizarre from my friends' angle.

"Yeah, but she must be a *white* witch!" Shaunna sniggers, tugging at a hunk of my not golden, not honey-coloured, not platinum, but wishy-washy milk-white blonde hair.

Hilarious – I don't think.

"You two take the mickey if you want. All I know is that a lot of strange things have happened today and it all has to mean *something*, doesn't it?"

"What – the fact that your mum gave you a biscuit instead of toast for breakfast, you think that's a cosmic event, do you?" says Shaunna, studying me hard.

"It's not that! It was the way that it all linked together! You know *exactly* what I mean!"

Course she did. So did Jude. OK, so the odd coincidence can make you go "hmm". In fact, the odd coincidence – like four red cars in a row driving by – can shoot right over your head, before you've even registered it properly. But a whole run of coincidences, like I'd just had . . . they couldn't just happen for no reason, could they?

You want evidence? OK. . .

To start with, before I woke up this morning I'd had this brilliant dream that I was out in some huge green field, twirling round and round, arms outstretched, gazing into the clear blue sky and feeling totally blissed out. Which was a weird dream to have considering I was totally stressed out last night, trying to cram like crazy for my maths exam today (and failing miserably). Then, in my dream, there's suddenly a huge, sparkly, sun-dappled shower of cooling rain – even though there's not a cloud in the sky. As I feel the droplets splash on my face I start laughing and twirling faster and faster, until—

The radio alarm clock came on, blasting out that feel-good Travis song, "Why Does It Always Rain On Me?".

See what I mean?

Next, I'm getting dressed, and something makes me think of the gold heart locket my gran gave me years ago. I've hardly ever worn it – it's not exactly as trendy as the jewellery and stuff I'm usually into. But this morning, I had this really strong feeling that I should wear it for luck. The only trouble was, I'd no idea where it could be, and I didn't have time to rummage around for it, if I wanted to get to school and the dreaded exam on time. It was then that I noticed the goofy-looking kink that had appeared in my hair overnight – a pony-tail was the only thing that was going to rescue me quickly from a hair disaster, but I couldn't find any of my usual black scrunchies lying around. I started yanking open the drawers in this cute wooden box thing I got from IKEA, and there was a pale blue scrunchie I've never worn – right on top of a red velvet box that held Gran's gold heart locket. . .

After that, the coincidences came thick and fast.

When I got down to breakfast, my little sister Mia gave me a handmade Good Luck card that she'd put together using pale blue paper folded over, with a heart drawn on in gold metallic ink.

Like every other exam day morning, I knew I was too nervous to eat anything, and hoped

Mum wouldn't give me her usual "but you can't do an exam on an empty stomach!" rant, not this morning. And she didn't. Instead of trying to tempt me with toast or cereal, she handed me one of those energy bars. "There's no point nagging you today," she laughed. "Not since it's the last exam. Just try and eat a bit of that on the way to school."

I was about to leave the house when I had this sinking realization that Dad didn't wish me luck before I went to bed last night – he'd have left for work already, and that felt wrong somehow. "Hi, Molly!" he surprised me by saying, as I opened the front door. "Left without my notes. What an idiot! Anyway, good luck for today, eh?!"

And with that, I walked smiling towards the bus stop, squinting against the sun and wishing I'd brought my shades with me. But as soon as I thought that, a few specks of light rain sprinkled out of nowhere, making me grin as my dream came flooding back to me.

On the bus, I sat daydreaming and gazing out of the window, still watching the strangely sunny rain sprinkle down, when I realized we were going nowhere fast; and getting stuck in a huge, long traffic jam wasn't great news, since I couldn't afford to be late. Just as I felt myself frowning, sensing my inexplicable good mood start to slip away, I realized the bus had stopped right beside a giant billboard, advertising some kind of insurance or something. But apart from the name of the company at the bottom, all that was written on the billboard, in letters half a metre high, was *"Everything is going to be all right!"*

And with a lurch of the bus (and my heart) we were moving again, and I knew that I was going to make it to school on time, but only just. As soon as the bus pulled up at my stop, I ran like lightning for the main door, but before I got the chance to yank it open, the sun bounced off the glass door panel, and for a fleeting second, I could see my reflection surrounded by a halo of rainbow-tinted light.

And in that second – don't ask me why or how – I knew that everything was going to be all right. This series of coincidences; this was my "cosmic clue". Suddenly, all the things that had been worrying me and bugging me the last couple of weeks just didn't matter any more. Like these exams that've been giving me a premature ulcer. . .? I'm going to pass them OK, I just know it. The summer. . .? Something will come up; I won't be sitting twiddling my thumbs while my friends earn bucketloads of money.

And the stuff with Dean. . .? That'll be all right too, for sure.

Call me a freak, but I'm positive that Fate is – very kindly – trying to tell me to quit worrying. Thank you, Fate. . .

"Hey, what's that famous psychic called again? The one with the black hair and crossed eyes?"

"Mystic Meg," Jude helps Shaunna out.

"Mystic Meg – that's right! And we've got our very own Mental Molly!"

"Thanks for listening with an open mind, Shaunna," I flip a silly, sarky comment back to her. "Wait till Dean hears the names you've been calling me; he'll— *eek!*"

My bare feet are suddenly being tickled, and unless Jude and Shaunna have grown exceptionally long arms, I can't pin the blame on them.

"Who's been calling you what names?" says Dean, appearing out of nowhere and dropping on to his knees beside me and my friends.

He presents me with a buttercup – the instrument of my tickling torture.

"Hi! What are you doing here?" I quiz him, sitting bolt upright now.

In spite of my daily (and nightly) head tangles about the two of us, I'm as glad as ever to see him and in no hurry to answer his question.

 14

"Just thought I'd come and meet you from school as a surprise, Mol. But I didn't realize you'd have finished your exam already."

"How did you know to find us here?" Jude asks him, elbows buried in the grass, propping up her head with her hands.

"I didn't. I don't know what made me decide to cut through the park, really. But here I am. And then, of course, I heard you lot laughing. . ."

I turn round and raise my eyebrows at my girl-friends. Do they need any more proof?

"Don't start!" Shaunna smirks, waggling a finger in my face.

"What's going on?" Dean asks, confused, and knowing he's stumbled into the middle of something. (Into the middle of a whole *bundle* of coincidences.)

"Don't take any notice of her, Dean," Shaunna informs him brightly. "Molly's gone all 'Hello trees, hello sky!' hippy-dippy on us today."

"Hey, I think I like the sound of that!" Dean grins, linking the fingers of one hand around mine.

I notice a tiny, flyaway, buttercup petal on his fingernail. It's a funny shape; like a perfect golden-yellow heart.

With my free hand, I reach up and touch the locket around my neck.

"Want to hear about my weird day?" I smile at Dean.

"Sure . . . but do you want to get out of here first?" he asks, staring into the sunny sky. "It feels like it's starting to rain. . ."

I think Dean – not to mention Shaunna and Jude – is quite surprised when I leap to my feet and start twirling and laughing, arms out-stretched, feeling the raindrops on my face.

Bonkers? Yes. But it has been a bonkers, blissed-out kind of day. . .

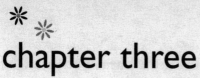

chapter three
Fate, milk, and me...

Date: *Friday 22nd June*

Frame of mind: *Delirious*

Twists of Fate: *One, thanks to Dad and large amounts of lager...*

"Hi! Would you like a leaflet on the health benefits of milk?"

"Hi! Would you like to try a sample carton of strawberry milkshake? No – don't worry, it's free!"

"Hi! Here's a money-off voucher for ice-cold milk – the stall's right over there! That's OK, you're welcome!"

That's all me, practising the lines in my head for my (*maybe*, potential, fingers-crossed) summer job, when I guess I should really be listening to what's being said. Maybe I need to remind myself that I'm still in the interview – I haven't *got* the thing yet.

"Sorry?" I smile, hoping I haven't blown it.

"I said, do you think you like the sound of it?" asks the interviewer, his hands resting on his trendy dirty-look, dark denims.

Do I like the sound of it?! I like the sound of it so much I can hardly find the *words* to say how much I like the sound of it.

And speaking of sounds, I see the young guy in front of me frown slightly and glance around the room for the source of the small but frantic thud-thud-thudding noise. Immediately I slap my hand down on my leg to stop it jittering up and down. How thrilled am I?

"Mmm, yes – it all sounds . . . fine!" I find myself beaming, hoping I look confident, assured and enthusiastic. (Instead of desperate, delirious and on the verge of *whooping* with excitement.)

The young guy perched on the edge of his desk looks like he should be standing behind a DJ console, not interviewing me for a summer job (maybe it's the trendy jeans and RayBans). Still, I don't care what he looks like (OK, he's cute, in a poseur-ish way) – all I'm interested in is the fact that this job sounds like heaven with a pay cheque.

I mean, two months of trundling around all the summer fêtes and fairs in the area, handing out leaflets and stuff, and smiling at people? It sure beats shelf-stacking at Tesco (like Jude) or table-wiping in the Tesco café (like Shaunna). It even beats Dean's job. Yes, so being a lifeguard at our local lido means you're guaranteed a tan, but then there *are* the hours and hours of sitting around hoping something interesting happens that doesn't involve anyone drowning. . .

Hey, you know what? I was absolutely, positively, *spookily* certain something would come up for me. Didn't I say that? Didn't I read that in my horoscope? Didn't I think that a week or so ago, when I had my weird day of coincidences, back when I was doing my maths exam? And now here I am, in the offices of this flash marketing company, hoping I'm impressing this bloke enough to be chosen as one of the promotional people for his clients (some big dairy conglomerate), and trying *really* hard to stop my foot from drumming again.

Oh, *please* let me get this job . . . *please* let me get this job. . .

"Well, Molly, thanks for coming," says the trendy bloke, sticking out a hand for me to shake. "I'll let you know."

Damn. I hope he doesn't feel how trembly and damp my stupid hand is. *What* a giveaway.

"Great!" I beam broadly at him, standing up straight and resisting the urge to throw myself at his feet and *beg* for the job. . .

"So, tell us about the job, then," says Shaunna. "What exactly does a Milk Promotions Assistant actually do?"

I've just come to celebrate the end of my first proper interview with Shaunna and Jude, who – I was pleased to see when I arrived all of thirty seconds ago – had bagsied one of the best tables in the mall café. It's right by the railings and overhangs the shopping concourse below: excellent for people-watching (i.e. bitching about bad-taste fashions without any fear of being overheard and thumped).

"Well," I start to explain, "there's going to be this mobile milk van thing that gets driven around all the county fairs and events, and it doubles as a stall, where they'll sell milk and milkshakes. So, the marketing company are hiring a couple of older people with driving licences to take care of

 20

getting the van around, and to man the stall. Then they want a couple of younger people to go out in the crowds and hand out leaflets and everything. And that's me."

"What – so you just mooch around, chatting to people all day?" Jude asks.

"Basically, yeah."

"Sounds fun. . ."

Shaunna sounds suddenly flat, which isn't fair really. For one thing, I haven't got the job yet (it's not like they're going to phone me in the next five minutes and say, "Hello, Miss Palmer, we'd love to offer you the job!"); and for another thing, Shaunna has to remember what a kick in the teeth it was for me when we all applied to Tesco for summer jobs and I didn't even get an *interview*. That felt like the *pits*. "They couldn't have got your application!" Mum had said, trying to soothe me, when I first heard that Shaunna and Jude had got through the selection procedure. "It's just one of those fluke things – they probably get so many applications, they just do a lucky dip!" Dean had said, shrugging. Both explanations could be true (I couldn't have made *that* much of a muck-up of a straightforward application form), but it didn't help me feel any less worthless at the time.

21

Shaunna's one of my best mates; I don't want her of all people going all jealous on me. And I can't exactly help it if Fate stepped in and gave me a nudge in the right direction, just when I needed it, can I?

"Listen, me getting this interview – it was just one of those coincidence things!"

As soon as I say this, Shaunna groans and mumbles, "Here we go!"

"What do you mean, Mol?" asks Jude, frowning over her clinking glass of iced Coke.

Good, at least *someone* seems vaguely interested in what I've got to say. 'Cause it's true – me finding out about this job was just as much a case of flukey coincidence as anything that had happened to me last Thursday.

"All this is down to my dad," I tell Jude.

"Yeah, I remember you saying something about that. But how does the coincidence thing come into it again?"

"Well, Dad went out on a work's night out last week, drank too much beer and had a horrible hangover next day," I say patiently, although I've told her and Shaunna this already – I just don't think they took the fate factor seriously. "He was supposed to ring some guy somewhere about something to do with work, but because he was a bit fuzzy-headed, he pressed the wrong speed-dial button and ended up speaking to an old mate who'd left the company a while ago to start up a marketing company."

"Whoo-OO-oo! A marketing company – how *weird*!" Shaunna teases me.

"*Anyway*," I continue, ignoring her. "Dad gets talking, and by the end of the conversation, this bloke's telling Dad about the latest client they've got on board, and that it's a nightmare 'cause they've got to find summer staff for them in about two seconds flat. And then Dad mentions me, and . . . well, I got the interview."

"Yeah, I *know* all that, but what's it got to do with coincid— oh, *I* get it!" Jude suddenly clicks. "If your dad hadn't been *hungover*, he wouldn't have pressed the *wrong* button, and he *wouldn't* have—"

"Blah, blah, blah!" Shaunna laughs, rolling her finger along in the air as the truth of my story dawns on Jude.

"God, I suppose that *is* weird!"

Jude blinks in amazement at me. Hey, I'm pretty amazed at the whole turn of events myself.

"Look, I hate to interrupt a beautiful cosmic moment between you two," says Shaunna. "But if you want a really *spooky* chain of coincidences, *I've* got one!"

"Oh, yeah?"

I narrow my eyes at Shaunna. Somehow I feel I'm probably just about to be the butt of *more* Mental Molly jokes. . .

"Uh-huh. Get this: yesterday, the sun was shining. . ."

Um, yeah. It *is* June.

". . .and then I switched on the TV, and there was the weather girl, pointing to the seaside and slapping a great big 'sun' symbol on it. . ."

Where is Shaunna going with this exactly?

". . .and then the *next* programme on was a holiday thing, all about sunny beach resorts in Britain. Isn't that amazing?"

Shaunna is holding her palms up – all innocence – her long, dark hair tumbling around her face. She's up to something and I can't quite figure out what.

"Huh?"

Jude has scrunched her face up in total confusion.

"And *then*. . ." Shaunna continues, knowing she's got our full attention, ". . .then this morning I pass a travel agent's, and in the window is this brochure with a big sun on it, and I'm spookily drawn inside, towards it. . ."

She's *seriously* taking the mick now, I can tell.

 24

". . .and here it is!"

In a nano-second, Shaunna has reached in her bag and yanked out a slightly crumpled brochure that (sure enough) has a sun on it, as well as a picture of a caravan, a sunset and a long, long beach.

"So?" I ask, after studying it for clues to her joke.

"So . . . at the very end of the summer holidays, just before the new school term starts," Shaunna grins wildly, hardly able to contain her excitement, "how about us three having a long weekend here? As a treat for having worked the whole summer? It's only an hour away by train, so our parents shouldn't flip. And it's a caravan, so it's pretty much dead cheap. What d'you think?"

What do I think? I like the sound of it so much I can hardly find the *words* to say what I think.

Funny . . . this summer's just getting better and better, even though it was looking pretty much *tragic* two weeks ago, when I was still in the midst of exam trauma, no-job hell, and the stuff with Dean.

Actually, technically-speaking, I'm *still* in no-job hell (*and* I still haven't found the right time to talk to Dean). No-job hell means no money, but *surely* I could come up with enough to go away with my friends on our first parent-free holiday ever. Somehow I could scrape together—

It's my mobile that's ringing. Actually, it's always dead easy to work out whose phone it is when the three of us are together: Shaunna's ringtone is "Teenage Dirtbag", Jude's is The Beatles' "Hey Jude" (but of course), and mine is the theme tune to *Bagpuss*. Yes, sad, I know.

"Just a sec!" I interrupt the rampant conversation that's *just* about to bubble up between the three of us, now that Shaunna's holiday suggestion has sunk in. "Hello?"

Shaunna and Jude look frozen in the moment, desperate with excitement, but on hold while I take this call.

"Oh . . . right," I nod at the voice talking to me – just as keen as my friends to get back to the holiday gossip. "Yes . . . that would be lovely. Yes . . . definitely. Thanks – thanks for letting me know. Uh-huh. . . OK. . . No problem. Bye!"

"Well?" Shaunna frowns at me.

"Well. . ." I find myself shaking, remembering what I thought to myself less than ten minutes ago – the thing about it hardly being likely that denim-and-shades man would be calling me back imminently. "I. . . I got the job! I start in a couple of weeks!"

The three of us are simultaneously shrieking so much that everyone in the shopping-centre café – make that in the whole of the shopping centre (the parking attendant in the attached multi-storey car park probably just lost his eardrums) – spins around to check we haven't been accidentally electrocuted or dropped in a vat of snakes or something.

Thank you, Fate . . . maybe Shaunna and Jude think I'm a freak for believing in you, but I'm just happy that I've got a) brilliant friends, b) a great job, and c) a better summer than I thought I'd ever have.

Wow, how blissed out can a girl get?

At this rate I might just have to write Fate a thank-you letter. Once I get the thing with Dean sorted out, of course. . .

chapter four

Not quite, but nearly...

Date: 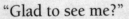 *Wednesday 3rd July*

Frame of mind: *Glad and sad*

Twists of Fate: *One that isn't going to please everyone...*

"Glad to see me?"

"Of course," I smile at Dean via the mirror. "It's funny, I was just thinking about you, right before you rang the doorbell."

"What – Mental Molly has one of her amazing premonitions?"

Great. Nice to know he's having fun teasing me, just like Shaunna and Jude. (Yeah, Jude's little glimmer of understanding after my interview soon evaporated. She's back to making *Scooby Doo* ghost noises every time I vaguely mention any of this fate stuff.)

But how do they explain the fact that my parents were unexpectedly fine about this whole weekend-by-the-sea business? Which came about purely because my mum's boss at work had just told Mum that her similarly-aged daughter did exactly the same thing last summer. She went on to say that letting her go had improved the trust between them and their relationship in general. Mum mulled that one over and decided that she and Dad should give me the thumbs-up to our girls' weekend away. (Meanwhile, *I've* been mulling it over and have decided I owe my mother's boss one *big* bunch of flowers.)

I don't care what Dean or Shaunna or Jude says – that was a *huge* coincidence. And here's another one – Dean dropping by just when I was thinking that I needed to solve the last bit of the puzzle. With everything else slotting into place and pointing towards a great summer, this unspoken thing between us . . . it could spoil everything. Not just the summer; us too.

"Dean . . . um, there's something I wanted to

talk about," I squeak in a wobbly little voice, as I avoid his eyes and do my make-up in the mirror.

But it seems like Dean isn't in listening mode. He's in mucking-about mode.

"Come here, you!"

"Dean! Let me go!"

"Molly! I said, come here!" Dean laughs, leaning forward on the sofa and making another grab for me.

Dean is very persistent when he wants a kiss. But it's very hard to put your mascara on when someone's trying to snog you.

"I can't!" I say, dodging his lazily swung arm. "I'm going to be late meeting Shaunna and Jude!"

It's eleven a.m. In ten minutes, I'm supposed to be meeting the girls outside the travel agent's, and that's a fifteen-minute walk away. (*You* do the maths. . .)

OK: I've got to blurt this out now – and quickly – while Fate's given me this perfect moment. I've got to talk to Dean about that night my parents were out and we were supposed to be babysitting Mia. She'd been in bed hours, safely lost in sleep, while me and Dean were in my bedroom, dangerously close to actually. . .

I tell you, if I hadn't heard Mia calling out for a glass of water, I don't know how far we'd have gone (and I never knew I could get dressed so quickly).

Nothing's been like that between us since, but even before that one night, it felt as if we were working up to that moment for ages, as if it was only a matter of time. And now – what's Dean thinking? . . .Expecting? That whenever we're babysitting again, we'll pick up right where we left off? Do *I* want that?

Yes. . .

No.

Maybe.

"Come on, then, what do you want to talk to me about?" Dean asks, sprawled on the sofa, dropping the jokes and staring seriously at my reflection in the mirror.

My heart's thundering again – I'm losing my bottle. Maybe I read the signs wrong . . . maybe this *isn't* the right time after all, not rushed, when I know Shaunna and Jude will be waiting for me.

"Save it – it's not important, I've *really* got to get a move on. Look, it's gone eleven. Shaunna and Jude'll kill me!" I state nervously, steadying one hand as I comb browny-black mascara on to my otherwise invisible eyelashes.

"*Aaaaagghhhhh!*"

Just when I think Dean's finished with the fooling around, I feel myself being suddenly rugby-tackled on to the sofa.

31

"Dean!" I squeal, trying to push him off me and not succeeding. "I could have poked my eye out with this mascara wand!"

I don't really give a toss about the mascara – I just feel out of control all of a sudden, and acting casual seems the best way to deal with it.

"No, you couldn't," he grins, millimetres away from my face, "that was a precision rugby-tackle – I knew *exactly* what I was doing."

"Yeah – making me late is what you're doing!" I force a smile, trying to break free again.

"Molly. . ."

I stop struggling for a second and look into his face. He's got the sweetest smattering of freckles across the bridge of his nose, like someone dotted them on with a kid's paintbrush.

"What?"

I think I'm going to have a heart attack, I really do. It's just occurred to me; here we are, all alone. We're not babysitting, we're not in my room, but. . .

"I'm not letting you up till you tell me you love me," Dean says with a smile, all his freckles disappearing into crinkles on either side of his nose.

I feel my muscles relax into mush. He's still just goofing around. That's OK. We do not have a situation here. It's business as usual, folks. . .

"You know I love you!" I say.

And I do love him, I really do. But it still feels like something's *changed*.

"Tell me again! I like it!"

"Dean – I told you, I love you, but not when you're deliberately making me late!"

"Aw, that's not fair!" Dean pretends to huff. "I love you . . . *all* the time. *No* exceptions."

Then again, maybe things *haven't* changed: maybe I'm making this whole thing ten times more complicated in my head than it really is. (Bet that's what Shaunna would say.) Maybe the best way to deal with this is to pretend it never happened. (Is that what Dean's doing?) Then, we could just go back to how we were. . .

"And you know all those gorgeous girls that'll be at the lido this summer?" Dean continues. "The ones I'll be in charge of looking after? . . .It'll be *your* face I'll be seeing when I'm giving them the kiss of life. . .!"

That's it. I'm not the jealous type (well, except for the time when Shaunna was dating Dean), but I've had enough of being teased. After all, I've got friends to meet, I've got a holiday to book. . .

"Let me go, Dean!" I order him, widening my eyes, and hitting him on the head with the nearest sofa cushion.

"*God*, Miss Palmer, you're *beautiful* when you're

angry!" he mutters in a stupid, hammy-actor way. "You're even beautiful when you do your make-up in that *wild, crazy* way!"

"*What* wild, crazy way?" I frown, stopping struggling for a second.

Dean is cracking up now, and flops back into a sitting position, letting me go.

Immediately, I bounce up and bound over to the mirror. . .

Hmm.

One eye is bare (a blue dot of iris surrounding by white eyeball, white eyelashes and white skin), while the other has browny-black upper eyelashes and an accompanying zigzaggy line of mascara right down my cheek.

"Sorry!" says Dean, holding out a box of Kleenex like a peace offering.

"I expect severe grovelling for this!" I tell him almost-sternly, while spitting on a tissue and scrubbing at my face, granny-style.

I feel giggly and almost light-headed with relief, really I do. We're just going to carry on, as if nothing's ever happened. As if that *night* never happened.

"Grovelling . . . I can do grovelling!" Dean announces, dropping to his knees and grabbing my knee.

"I said grovel – not wobble!" I say, grinning, trying once again to steady my hand and get some colour on to my eyelashes (and preferably nowhere else on my face).

"Sorry. Sorry . . . sorry . . . sorry," he mutters, making things ten times worse by pecking fluttery butterfly kisses on the back of my knee.

"DEAN!" I half-laugh, half-shout, half-enjoying it, and half-being driven mad. "I *have* to get out of here – about ten minutes ago!"

"Yeah, OK," Dean gives in, letting go of my leg and rolling backwards so he's sitting on the floor, weight resting on his arms, eyes gazing up at me. (It's funny to feel adored, but that's what Dean makes me feel.)

"What?" I smile down at him, wondering what this new, more serious, tentative look is all about.

"Molly . . . I, um. . ." he murmurs. "Well, it's just that last night: I got thinking, and – and there's something I want to ask you. . ."

"Oh?" I say nervously, feeling myself smudge my mascara all over again.

"Where've you been?" Jude demands, her skinny arms tangled up, more origami'd than simply crossed.

"Yeah, don't mind *us*!" Shaunna says. "We've only been waiting for you for *ever*..."

"She means five minutes!" Jude turns, about to lead the way into the travel agent's now that I've finally arrived.

"Um ... hold on a second," I mutter, small-voiced.

"Huh?" Jude and Shaunna turn back and say as one, both staring at me from the doorstep of the shop.

Inside, I can see one bored-looking sales assistant wondering whether he's about to make some commission on us, or if we're just time-wasting teenagers. Well, I can't speak for Jude and Shaunna, but that sales assistant sure isn't going to be making any commission out of *me* today.

"It's ... it's mine and Dean's anniversary," I mumble pathetically, not knowing where to start and how exactly to sugar-coat what I'm about to say.

"Already?" Shaunna frowns, her mind obviously whirring back to last summer and her own time dating Dean. She's about to tell me I've got my facts wrong when I take another stab at explaining myself.

"No ... I mean at the end of the summer. September first," I say, wishing and hoping

Shaunna and Jude could mind-read all of a sudden and make this whole explanation thing a lot easier for me.

"That's, um, *nice*. . ." says Jude dubiously, smiling and frowning at me at the same time, and obviously bewildered by what I'm trying to say.

"It's just. . ."

I'm looking at my two bemused friends and suddenly I lose my bottle (for the second time today). I bury my head in my hands and mumble out the words.

". . .it's just that I can't come on holiday with you guys."

"*What!*"

I move my fingers *just* enough to peer at my friends though the gaps. It's my chicken version of hiding behind the sofa during a scary video.

"I can't come with you. Dean's asked me to go away with him that weekend, 'cause it's our one-year anniversary."

By the look on Jude and Shaunna's faces, you'd think that I'd just told them I'd deliberately run over a cat in the road.

This is bizarre: fifteen minutes ago, Dean made me the happiest girl in the cosmiverse by suggesting we go away together; and now, the flipside of it is I feel like the biggest scuzzbag in the world.

"Sorry. . ." I mutter, hanging my head low and feeling about the size of a slug.

I wait for one of my mates to tell me it doesn't matter – that it's OK, but funnily enough, the only thing I can hear apart from background traffic is one *huge* amount of guilt-tripping, echoing silence.

But what can I do? This morning – just like the last few weeks – I'd been trying to make sense of what was going on with Dean and me. And while I was busy being in a flap, Dean was working up to asking me to go to Ireland with him at the end of the holidays, which totally took my breath away. Neither of us said anything, but we both know what it means . . . and by that time, there'll be no more yes, no, maybes muddling around in my head. It'll be perfect.

The last piece of the puzzle has fallen into place. My brilliant summer starts here. . .

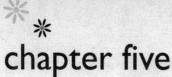

chapter five

Fancy an aura-cleansing, madam?

Date: *Saturday 13th July*

Frame of mind: *Spiritual(ish)*

Twists of Fate: *Small, flowery, wordy ones...*

This morning, before I left the house, a big bouquet of red roses, gypsophila and ivy was delivered to the door – my dad's idea of surprising Mum for their anniversary.

My sister Mia and I both said, "Ooh, they're *beautiful!*" at exactly the same time, with exactly the same intonation. Then Mia watched me put on my new lip gloss and mentioned that the colour looked exactly like the roses in Mum's bouquet. Out of curiosity, I flipped the lip-gloss container over to see what the colour was called: 'Rose Rouge'. But of course. . .

It gave me warm chills, if there is such a thing. Then I met up with Shaunna and Jude, and right now I'm getting cold chills, thanks to the way Shaunna's acting up. Honestly, she's been getting worse lately – and I'm sure it's down to her dating Dean's cousin, Adam Pindar. Adam's the funniest guy I know, but he always goes too far to get a laugh and that's what Shaunna's like a lot of the time now.

"So what do you reckon – do you think my aura needs cleansing or not?"

Shaunna stares enquiringly at me and Jude while wafting her hands a few centimetres from either side of her head and humming the theme tune to *The X-Files*. Somehow, the woman in purple velvet and multiple crystal necklaces manning the "Cleanse Your Aura" stall doesn't seem to appreciate Shaunna being so flippant.

"Come on!" I hiss, as I make a grab for Shaunna's sleeve and drag her away so that we can escape the stallholder's icy glare amongst the thronging crowds.

"Although *normally*," Shaunna continues

unperturbed (and loudly), "I find Pantene cleanses my aura – and my hair – quite nicely, *and* it doesn't cost twenty-five quid a time!"

Jude isn't helping. She's giggling so hard that she's given herself hiccups.

"Let's go this way – we haven't checked out these stalls," I suggest, gently shoving my friends in the direction of a slightly less busy aisle. Not that it's going to help matters any. They'll only find new things to snigger at. I don't know why they wanted to come to this Alternative World of Well-Being Fair at all, if they're not going to take it seriously. We paid a fiver each to get in here, and that's a lot of money to fork out if all you're going to do is laugh yourself stupid at all the New Age-y therapies on offer.

OK, so I'm guilty of doing that a bit too. I *did* find it hard not to crack up when we passed the "Come and Hum for Peace!" stand. It's just that the vision of half-a-dozen members of the public being jollied into a hum-a-long to John Lennon's "Imagine" by a small, fat, bald guy in a toga, bobbly socks and sandals is a pretty hard thing to watch and keep a straight face, especially when no one seemed to be able to keep in tune (or even *know* the tune).

But I've been really interested in lots of the

other stuff on show, specially after the weirdly wonderful month of coincidences *I've* just had. So far, I've bought a Native American Dream-Catcher ("*Mug*-Catcher, more like. *How* much did you pay for that thing?" Shaunna said); a piece of amethyst quartz crystal ("It's supposed to 'purify ideas'?" frowned Jude. "But how can it? It's just a stone. A very *pretty* stone, but. . ."); and picked up a bunch of leaflets on stuff like *Expand Your Psychic Potential* and *Colour Therapy – How it Can Change Your Life*.

All Jude has bought today is a veggie burger, and the only leaflet Shaunna's picked up is called *Feet – A Signpost of Spirituality*, which she thinks Adam will find a real hoot since he just got a verruca burnt off yesterday.

"Hey! *Now* you're talking!" says Shaunna, sprinting away from us and nabbing herself a free try-out on a vibrating massage chair.

"Does it feel good?" I ask a gently wobbling Shaunna, who's lying back in the seat with her eyes closed and a blissed-out expression on her face. It's the first time she's stopped sniggering in forty-five minutes.

"Ye-e-e-e-e-s-s-s!" her voice warbles in reply.

Some more people push in and gawp at the massage chairs and the testers all being happily jiggled in them. Since these people seem older than us and look as if they might feasibly have enough money in their bank accounts to buy one of these things, Jude and I step aside. Despite having summer jobs starting in two days' time, me and Jude – skint sixteen year olds that we are – definitely *don't* happen to have a spare few hundred pounds to fritter away on massage chairs.

"It's like something out of *Nightmare On Elm Street*," Jude mutters dubiously, watching strange lumps and bumps moving around under the material of the chair Shaunna is reclining on. "It looks like it's going to swallow her!"

"Good!" I say, grinning. "Maybe that means I get to see the rest of the fair in peace!"

Jude says nothing for a second, then turns around and stares at me.

"Are you OK, Molly?" she asks tentatively.

"Yeah! Of course! Why shouldn't I be?"

Course I'm happy enough. Even though Jude and Shaunna (especially Shaunna) are working my nerves a little this afternoon, I'm still really chuffed to see them. After all, things have been a bit frosty between us all over the last week or so, after me dropping the bombshell that I was going on holiday with Dean instead of them. Until today,

I hadn't seen either Jude *or* Shaunna since we'd met up outside the travel agent's. Yeah, we'd spoken on the phone, but they'd both seemed too busy with stuff (stuff like not seeing me) for us to get together like normal. So when Shaunna had phoned up and suggested that the three of us have a day out at this alternative health fair, I was very happy. It's like my penance is over – it seems like the girls have forgiven me (even if they haven't actually said so out loud).

"Well," says Jude, biting nervously at her thumbnail, "what's wrong is that *you* seem to have had a sense of humour bypass this afternoon. . ."

I'm about to tell her she's wrong; that my sense of humour is just where it's always been and doing fine, thanks, when I realize she's right.

"So?" Jude asks, watching me open and then shut my mouth. "What's up, Mol?"

"It's this thing about going away on holiday with Dean," I blurt out.

"What about it? You're still going, yeah?"

"Well . . . *hopefully*. I just haven't got round to telling Mum and Dad yet. And I'm kind of dreading it."

"Ah!" Jude nods, seeing my point. "You're worried how they're going to react to the idea of their little girl sharing a big, double bed with Dean!"

I feel my face flush. God, it sounds so *seedy* when she puts it like that. And ever since Dean asked me to go away with him, the problem of how to break the news to Mum and Dad without the whole thing coming over all sordid has been festering away in the back of my mind. Actually, I nearly told Mum last night, when we started having this really good chat about life, the universe and what a nice boy Dean was. But then a minuscule piece of wood (in the form of a splinter in Mia's finger) came between us and spoiled the moment. Next thing, Mum's putting on her nurse's hat and I'm putting my secret back in its box. . .

"I just don't think they're going to be too thrilled at the idea, even though they really, really like Dean," I say.

Yep, this dread of telling my parents about our romantic, anniversary getaway . . . it's like that little black cloud of gloom has reappeared, hovering ominously on the horizon.

"Oh, wow!" roars Shaunna, suddenly popping up beside us. I assume she's wowing wide-eyed at the freebie armchair massage she's just had, but I'm wrong – she's pointing at a large stand at the bottom of this particular aisle. "Come on – we've got to do this!"

45

Me and Jude will have to put our chat on hold – the "this" we've got to do is have our fortune told.

Shaunna is pushing us towards a busy stand where various psychics are using tarot cards, runes, crystal balls and palms to peek into the lives of people like me. Only I don't need my life peeked into. I can't put it into words exactly (well, I *can*, but it tends to come out embarrassingly hippy-dippy and will just make Shaunna and Jude crack up at me again), but I've already had my "cosmic clues" about what's going on in my life this summer. To go searching for more seems greedy, or like I'm tempting fate or something.

"Listen, why don't you two go ahead and get readings done?" I tell Shaunna and Jude. "I'll have a wander round and get a coffee."

"No way, Mental Molly!" Shaunna smiles, intertwining her arm with one of mine, while Jude takes up a similar position on the other side of me. "For the last month you've been telling me and Jude that we should get into all this spooky stuff, so here we are!"

"And if *we're* going to get a reading done," says Jude, "you're definitely *not* wriggling out if it."

Doesn't seem like I'm wriggling anywhere, not now I've found myself book-ended. The only way

*❋ 46

out would be to arm-wrestle them to the ground. . .

"This is a very pretty locket, dear. Is it an heir-loom?" asks the mumsy-looking woman sitting opposite me.

I don't know what I expect a psychic to look like, but it's not this person. She has a bad frizzy perm, blue streaky eyeshadow, orangey lipstick and a beige cardie on. If I'd had a choice (which I didn't – you just get allocated the next palm/tarot-card/crystal-ball reader who's free), I think I'd have liked either of the women Jude and Shaunna have ended up with. Right at this moment, Shaunna is sitting with an unfeasibly pretty Asian woman, who's chucking coins and scribbling things, which is apparently I-Ching. Jude ended up with this Miss Haversham-style old lady with flowing white hair, eye-popping hunks of amber jewellery and a set of tarot cards.

Mrs Beige Cardie hasn't got any coins to chuck or cards to fan out. Mrs Beige Cardie believes in holding a personal object and getting visions. (I'm glad I've taken to wearing the heart-shaped gold locket lately, otherwise all I'd have been able to give her today is my mobile, and since they can mess up the radio frequencies in aeroplanes, who knows what they could do to psychic vibes. . .?)

"I, um, got it from my gran."

"Ah!" she smiles sagely. "I *knew* it was a family heirloom! You're *very* special to her you know!"

Um . . . should I set her straight? Should I tell her that I got it from my gran, who bought it for my twelfth birthday, from Argos? And that my gran wrote the label out "To Mia", since she constantly muddles up me and my sister (and our cousins for that matter)?

"So now, dear, let's see what we see. . ." says Mrs Beige Cardie, closing her eyes and giving me a better view of the waxy streaks of blue eyeshadow on her eyelids, and putting a stop to me doing any more explaining.

Wow – suddenly my heart's hammering dementedly. I like my coincidences; over the last month or so, they've been magical and comforting. But the idea that this woman (in a beige cardie) can somehow stare into my soul and into my future feels more than slightly freaky.

"Hmmm. . ." Mrs BC smiles beatifically. "I see I'm in the presence of a Taurean."

"Um, Virgo, actually."

"Of course!" she booms, unperturbed. "I sensed an Earth sign *straight* away!"

"Oh."

All of a sudden, I could almost hear Shaunna's voice of reason in my head; "Fire, Water, Earth, Air . . . she had a one-in-four chance of getting it right, didn't she?" As soon as I thought that thought, I chucked it straight out of my mind.

"You're at your best in the mornings, aren't you?" Mrs BC smiles, her eyes still shut and unseeing.

I don't know about that. I nearly used Toilet Duck instead of Timotei in the shower the other day, just 'cause I was still half-asleep.

"And that's because you were born in the morning!" the woman announces. "Am I right?"

"Uh . . . I think I was born at about three a.m."

"Yes – a mystical time, just before the sun rises. . ."

To be honest, I don't really know what she means. Hey, maybe I should set my alarm for three in the morning sometime – maybe I'd be surprised at how brilliant I feel. Then again. . .

"You're an only child," Mrs BC mutters on, as I watch her pupils dart back and forth beneath her eyelids, just like the mechanical knuckles that had moved underneath Shaunna in the massage chair.

"Er . . . I have a little sister," I correct her, wondering if I'm allowed to do that. (Will burly security guards come and haul me away for contradicting a psychic?)

"Yes, but she's a lot younger; too young to be close to you. Which is why you give off the *aura* of being an only child."

Oh. Aren't I close to Mia? I *thought* I was . . . but then she's only ten, so I guess you *could* say—

"Maybe, of course, the loneliness I sense is to do with love. Is that correct, dear?"

Mrs BC's eyes suddenly flip open and she stares disconcertingly hard into mine. I'm momentarily flustered. Is she about to talk about Dean? But what's that got to do with loneli—

"I can see that I'm right, dear!" Mrs BC beams. "From the way you're blushing I can tell I've hit a tender spot! Well, let me reassure you, what I'm getting from the other side is. . ."

She closes her eyes again and runs the heart-shaped locket through her fingers once more. It doesn't seem right to try and interrupt her right now. Confused, I touch my face and feel how hot it is. I'm blushing all right – blushing at the fact that my *initial* blush (caused by Mrs BC staring at me intensely) has just given this woman completely the wrong signals.

". . .is that you're going to go through a difficult time over the summer. . ."

What?!

". . .but you must be patient, because once your troubles are resolved. . ."

What troubles?

". . .you *will* find true love."

Actually, I've got love, thank you very much! I feel like saying, but chicken out.

"Well, there is someone – my boyfriend, Dean," I mumble, knowing I sound apologetic, although I'm not sure why.

"Well, as I say, there will be troubles in your life," says Mrs BC hurriedly, seemingly ignoring the mention of Dean.

"And . . . what are these *troubles* exactly?" I find myself tentatively asking.

"Well, dear, it's hard to say," Mrs BC frowns. "It's not very clear to see."

Hmm. How convenient.

"Ah! Here's something . . . something to do with jealousy . . . but, no . . . no, it's gone again."

"What? *I* get jealous of someone?" I ask dubiously, trying to get a handle on this. "Or someone gets jealous of *me*?"

"Oh, it's getting very hazy. . ." Mrs BC mumbles, starting to sway from side to side. "I can sense the spirits slipping away. . ."

Her eyelids flip open and she passes me my

locket, and starts fiddling with the buttons on her cardie.

"Sorry, dear. Sometimes the spirits are there and sometimes they're not. Tell you what; I'll knock a couple of pounds off my fee for you. How's that?"

That, is hopeless. And so is this fortune teller.

And I don't need any supernatural powers to tell me that Shaunna and Jude are going to get an *almighty* kick out of me coming across the crummiest, fakest so-called psychic in the Western hemisphere. . .

chapter six
Mmm … minging

Date: *Monday 15th July*

Frame of mind: *Bedazzled*

Twists of Fate: *A soggy, wet twist (thanks a lot, Fate)*

According to Saturday's fortune tellers, Shaunna is going to travel a lot ("Does that mean I get a job as a bus driver?") and Jude is going to have lots of babies ("Well, I like kids, but I couldn't eat a whole one!"). I was taking my own glimpse of the future (at least Mrs Beige Cardie's dubious version) with as big a pinch of salt as my friends were.

Although it *was* true that I was experiencing trouble already. . . I couldn't seem get any of my face muscles to work.

"Smile!"

"I can't!" I whimper.

"You've got to!"

"I *can't*, Cameron." I shake my head, wishing I'd brought my shades with me. Not just 'cause of the brightness of the day, but because gazing at Cameron or at my own reflection is likely to damage my retinas faster than staring directly into the sun ever could. White T-shirt; white trousers; brand-new, scuff-free, dazzling white trainers; stupid white hair. I feel as luminous as a strip-light.

"Yes, you *can*, Mol. Remember, smiling is part of our job description!"

I know he means it ironically (doesn't he?). Still, it doesn't make me feel any more inclined to stretch my mouth into action.

"But it's just that I feel like a right lemon in this get-up!" I mumble, clutching my why-milk-is-good-for-you leaflets and treading nervously towards the milling crowds at today's agricultural fair.

"You look fine! *We* look fine!"

I turn and stare incredulously at Cameron, my new work-mate (chosen – presumably – for his

54

cheesy-cute, blond-hair-and-round-glasses, Milky Bar kid looks). Me, with my milky-white hair, milky-white skin and this stuff I've been forced to wear: no guesses why *I* was chosen – I look exactly like a big glass of semi-skimmed. Why's he saying we look fine? He's got to be joking, right?

Right. (Phew. . .)

Cameron is grinning broadly, his eyes blinking mischievously at me from behind his penny rounder specs. Suddenly, it's glaringly obvious that he feels just as much of a lemon as I do in our matching all-white gear, only he's handling it better than me – i.e. laughing about it.

"But this T-shirt!" I moan, pulling it out at the waist and reading – upside-down – the logo emblazoned across my chest. "*Mmm . . . Milk!* It's *awful*! Who thought that up? My kid sister could come up with a better slogan than that!"

"I think the guy at the marketing company came up with it. Remember Simon? The one who gave us these jobs?"

"Oh, right," I grimace, getting his point. "Still, *Mmm . . . Milk!* Urgh!"

"Mol, just do what I'm doing and think of the mmm . . . *money* we're going to be making!" Cameron reminds me, giving me a hefty pat on the back.

55

He seems pretty funny, this lad, but as I only met him an hour ago – when we hooked up with Clare and Danielle (both in their thirties, both of whom look more ridiculous in their *Mmm . . . Milk!* T-shirts than me and Cameron, it has to be said) – it's hard to tell yet. On the drive out here from town, I was pretty glad of the lame jokes he kept coming out with, mainly 'cause they took my mind off the fact that I was a) nervous about my first day at work, and b) feeling kind of travel sick, the way Danielle was belting the Milk Mobile along the motorway at intergalactic speeds.

But I got the impression Clare and Danielle thought Cameron was pretty cocky; you know – the mouthy sixteen year old who doesn't shut up. You could tell that's what was trundling through their minds from the way both women exchanged glances when they thought neither of us were looking. (Tough luck that old hawkeye me spotted them.) I got annoyed for Cameron when I saw that – I mean, he *could* just have been prattling on 'cause he was nervous. But then, part of me thinks he *is* maybe a bit too full-on – the way he's started calling me "Mol" already, and the hefty thump on the back there, for example. Maybe it's just a little too buddy-buddy, touchy-feely for two people who hardly know each other. Then again, I should

 56

give him a chance – after all, I get the feeling that Clare and Danielle have already chummed up and lumped me in with Cameron as the dumb teenagers. I might as well have an ally too. . .

"Anyway, dopey as this logo is," Cameron mumbles through a teeth-gritted smile, as he hands out his first leaflets to an uninterested passing family, "at least it lets people know what it is we're trying to flog. If we were only wearing plain white T-shirts along with the rest of this get-up, they might think we were members of some weirdo cult."

True, I think. The white clothes and the scary smiles . . . if someone like that came walking my way, I'd tend to presume their leaflets were full of stuff about how God is really an alien cucumber or something.

"Listen," says Cameron, glancing over his shoulder. "I don't mean to spook you, but Clare and Danielle are keeping tabs on us. Maybe you'd better start handing out some of those leaflets, and maybe it's a good time to give that smiling thing a go!"

God, I'd better get myself together, or there'll definitely be no pay packet and no *mmm* . . . *money* at the end of the week for me. And what I've got to keep reminding myself of is that, hideous white clothes or not, I've got to be having an *infinitely* better day than Shaunna and Jude. I mean, who can complain about aimlessly wandering around in the sunshine, smiling a smile (once I get the hang of slapping it on my face), giving out leaflets and vouchers to a grateful public? Specially when I know the girls will be stuck indoors, wearing a naff uniform (Jude) or an even more naff apron (Shaunna), spending the next seven hours stacking toilet roll or wiping eggy dollops off plastic tables. I'm lucky and I'd better remember that. . .

"Hi! Like a money-off voucher for a milkshake?" I grin dumbly, as I thrust a leaflet into the hand of an elderly man smoking a pipe. Well, he might not be our target market, but a girl's got to start somewhere. . .

I wonder how Dean's getting on at the lido today? I muse, the thought of my boyfriend in his stupid, regulation short shorts bringing a more spontaneous smile to my face.

"Hi, there! Like a leaflet?" I beam, shoving one towards a harassed young mum who looks more in need of a lasso for her rampaging toddler than some blurb about the benefits of milk. Still, not my problem – I'm just doing my job.

OK, I think I'm loosening up a bit now. I can

see Cameron giving me an encouraging wink, as he wanders away from me, looking like an "after" shot in a get-your-whites-white! washing-powder ad campaign.

And maybe I should just get over this aversion to white. After all, when I was flicking through that colour therapy bumf I picked up at the alternative health fair on Saturday, I noticed that white is supposed to represent "calm, healing, vitality and spirituality". *That's* what I need to get into my head today. I need to concentrate on being calm, er . . . healing (hmm, maybe ditch that one for now), vital (is that the right word?) and spiritual.

"Do you know where the milkshakes are?" asks a small voice, as someone tugs at my T-shirt.

"Sure!" I smile, turning and gazing down at two small boys. "Here – take these vouchers and you get money off a milkshake at that stall over there. And if you ask nicely, they might even give you a free sample of—"

"'*Mmm . . . Milk!*'" one kid interrupts my sales patter, reading the slogan on my chest.

"That's right!" I say breezily. "Milk is very good for you; much better than fizzy—"

"And you're a big *mmm . . . MOO!*" yelps the other boy.

And before my eyes, the two little brats run off as fast as they can (which isn't very fast when you're bent double with giggles). All around me, there are people grinning at the charming cheek of the little tykes. The little tykes who I could now cheerfully hold down and force-feed strawberry milkshake until they barf. . .

Be calm! Be vital! Be spiritual! And SMILE! I remind myself of today's buzz words, as I glide on with my pride dented, but still intact, and aim a few leaflets into the crowd.

"Moo! *Moo!* Ha, ha, ha!"

I'll pretend I didn't hear that.

"Hey, Mol – you look like. . ."

"Whatever you're going to say, *don't* say it," I tell Cameron ruefully, as I bump into him on the way back to the Milk Mobile.

It's nearly four o'clock, it's nearly our official knocking-off time, and thanks to non-stop rain and a very un-July-ish cold wind breezing in, I think I've nearly got hypothermia.

"You look like one of those Cornetto ice creams."

"Meaning?" I shoot him a look through the soggy white curtains of hair that are stuck to either side of my face. I try and wipe them aside but I only end up slapping my face with my last few, floppy, soaked leaflets.

"From your knees up," Cameron points out, "you're vanilla ice-cream. From your knees down. . ."

". . .chocolate," I conclude wearily, staring down at the brown sludge of mud coating my new white jeans and trainers.

Actually, I feel like I'm wearing those giant platform Buffalo trainers the Spice Girls used to stumble on stage in, back in their early days. Below the soles of my nice-but-normal Nikes is a five-centimetre slab of sodden earth that I've managed to accumulate in the endless trudge I've made from the faraway other side of this godforsaken field of muddy gloop.

"So how come *you've* managed to stay dry?" I ask.

Not to mention clean, but I don't bother to tack that obvious statement on to my question to Cameron.

"I was right beside the vegetable-judging tent when the rain came on," he explains, pointing to the voluminous, warm-and-dry-as-toast marquee I've just passed. Lucky him – try being at the furthest away, shelter-free, downward-sloping point of a giant, football-pitch sized field when there's a torrential, freezing downpour, and you soon know about it. As do my nipples, which at this point are shaming me by standing out in alarmingly graphic detail.

Well, this is zero fun, I grumble in the privacy of my own head, as I speedily fold my arms across my chest.

Then, out of nowhere, I suddenly remember the dream I had last night . . . it was the same one I had right before my maths exam; the one about being in a field – all blue sky, green grass and sunshine – when the sparkly shower of rain starts sprinkling down on me, and I begin spinning around and around, laughing. Well, right now, I don't feel much like spinning. Or laughing. All I feel like doing is sinking into a deep, steaming, bubbly bath and washing off the half-a-field that's weighing down my jeans and soaking through to my legs.

There are only three words to describe how today's turned out, I think bleakly to myself. *And that's mmm . . . muddy, mmm . . . miserable and mmm . . . minging.*

What was it that fortune-teller said? About me having hassles this summer?

"Cheer up!" grins Cameron, wrapping an arm around my waist and giving me a squeeze. "It can't get any worse!"

You want a bet? I'm wet, freezing, filthy and have been the butt of endless teasing by small boys who've found it highly entertaining to follow me around all day *mooing*. If that wasn't enough, at the back of my mind is the promise I made to Dean that I'd absolutely, definitely, *finally* tell Mum and Dad about our holiday tonight (urgh. . .), and now some boy I hardly know is trying to paw me. Of *course* it can get worse.

"C'mere, Mol!" I hear Cameron urge me, as he wraps another arm around me and pulls me towards him.

OK – that's enough. I wrench myself free and step away from him . . . and straight into a firing line of mud that's spinning up from the wheels of a passing horse box.

"Nice. . ." I nod to myself, wiping splodges of wet brown earth from my face.

Now that I probably look like a cross between a Cornetto and a Dalmatian, all of a sudden, stacking toilet roll in Tesco's sounds pretty damn near perfect to me. . .

chapter seven

Shaunna, Jude ...
say hello to Fate

Date: *Monday 22nd July*

Frame of mind: *Indulgent*

Twists of Fate: *It's all in the stars...*

"What do you reckon?"

Shaunna holds her nails aloft. They are long. Very long. Shaunna is no girlie girl, and those are most definitely the girliest thing I've ever seen Shaunna in, except for the bridesmaid's dress she wore at her sister's wedding – but then she practically had to be forced into that at gunpoint.

These false nails; these ridiculously long pink nails . . . she's voluntarily *paid* to have those stuck on her fingers.

Weird.

"What I think is that they're going to ping off when you pick up your very first crate of baked beans," I tell her, studying the monstrosities at close quarters.

It's been fun today, having a full-on, girlie pamper-thon with Shaunna and Jude. It was my suggestion: to be honest, I'm still swilling in guilt from letting the girls down and spoiling the whole holiday thing, so I decided to suggest having ourselves a Day of Indulgence at the first opportunity our out of synch work shifts allowed. I got the idea from my horoscope this week: *"Friendships can wither if not well-tended. Put a bit of effort into yours, and you could be surprised at how much it's appreciated, and at the turn of events"*. I could do with that; a little appreciation, that is. After a week of handing out leaflets in unseasonal downpours, I get the feeling that the general public do not have any appreciation of how hard my job is (you can tell by how many leaflets end up strewn on the grass or stuffed in the litter bins), and my so-called lovely boyfriend Dean doesn't seem to appreciate just how hard it is to break bad news to my parents. But that's another story. . .

So today has been our Day of Indulgence, my day for "tending friendships", and it's been great. Me, Jude and Shaunna met at this greasy spoon caff first thing this morning, ordered double sausage, eggs and beans, and raced to see who could finish first. (Shaunna won – but then Jude spotted the sausage she had clenched between her knees and we realized she'd been cheating.) Then we went for a sauna at the new health and fitness studio that's opened in town, 'cause Simon represents them too, and he had handed out some freebie guest passes when he came to check up on us at the Arlington Steam Fair last week. That was a laugh (the sauna, I mean – not the Arlington Steam Fair, which was a rain-soaked, crowd-free disaster).

I don't think us lot being there was so much of a laugh for the other women in the sauna, who all seemed to leave pretty quickly (tutting loudly). I don't know what their problem was exactly, but I think it might have had something to do with Shaunna trying to sit all quietly and serious on one wooden bench, and then getting the giggles as soon as she looked over at me and Jude. And those giggles were pretty infectious. . .

Then – shazam! – it was time for food again, after sweating and giggling off a few calories at the posh health club. Jude suggested that since it was our official Day of Indulgence, we should ignore all sensible rules of nutrition and just eat cake. Smart thinking – specially since we'd started the day with a breakfast of nutrient-free grease and tomato sauce and not much else. So, after strawberry tarts, blackcurrant cheesecake, key lime pie, chocolate brownies and a crème caramel, we ended up here – in the nail salon in the shopping mall – feeling slightly queasy. As did the salon assistants when they caught sight of our mud-encrusted/work-chipped/stress-bitten nails. Me and Jude just had our raggedy efforts filed short and French manicured, but Shaunna had a brainstorm and forked out for the falsies.

"You'll need a whole new wardrobe to go with those," Jude nods down at Shaunna's waggling fingers. "They don't really go with your flared jeans and 'Ash' T-shirt."

"You're right!" says Shaunna, slapping her hands down on the counter and rattling the bottles of nail polish beside her. "Molly, get my money out of my jeans' pocket and pay the lady. We've got some serious shopping to do!"

Shaunna leaps up and sticks her bottom out towards me. Oh, well, anything for a friend. . .

The wall between the changing room and the main Ladieswear retail floor of Partington's department store is pretty thick, but I'm sure I can feel the X-ray, heat-seeking death glare of the snooty assistant manning the till out there.

"I'm sure she's going to come in and ask us to leave," I whisper urgently, in the echoey main area of the changing room.

"Don't worry about *her*," Shaunna shrugs, straightening the hat she's plonked on my head. "We could be rich little It girls, with Daddy's platinum card in our back pockets, ready to spend, spend, spend!"

"Except we're not," Jude points out, coming out from behind her cubical curtain and looking plainly ridiculous in a Spandex, leopard-skin-print halterneck dress with matching fringed bolero.

"Nasty!" Shaunna nods approvingly. "Cost?"

"Three hundred, give or take five pence."

Shaunna and Jude might be getting into this game of dressing up, but I'm still jumpy.

"Hey, that saleswoman – she *must* know we're just mucking around in here!"

"Listen, Mol – it's like Adam's always saying to me; act confident, and people *think* you're confident."

With that, Shaunna swivels me around by the shoulders to face the floor-to-ceiling mirror.

"Wow – *very* retro '80s," Jude comments, giving me the once-over. "*Love* the shoulder pads. And that giant floral print is *so* you, Mol."

I am standing in my bare feet, wearing a mother-of-the-bride satin two-piece suit, with so much sponge in the shoulders that I look deformed. In fact, I look like I've been swallowed by an old-fashioned, winged, chintz armchair.

"It's the hat that *makes* the outfit," Shaunna says dryly, as she rubs thoughtfully at her chin with her fingers.

The hat is a small turquoise dome with large, turquoise feathers sticking out of it, presumably plucked from the lesser-spotted turquoise bird.

"What are you guys *doing* to me!" I groan at my reflection.

"Bringing out the inner you. . .!"

"Yeah, but *you* still win, Shaunna!" says Jude. "Yours is *definitely* the worst outfit in the whole store. How much did you say it was?"

Shaunna twists round and practically bends herself double to check out the dangling price tag.

"Seven hundred and thirty quid."

"God – who knew bad taste could cost so much?" I marvel, staring at the Barbie-pink sequinned mini-dress that's slashed from the neck to the navel for maximum cleavage exposure.

"I like the way you've accessorized it with an off-white bra and Converse flip-flops," Jude comments.

"And unshaved legs, don't forget!"

This was all Shaunna's idea, of course. Invade the hallowed space of Partington's Ladieswear department – otherwise known as the Middle-Aged Ladies With Too Much Money And No Taste department – and have a contest to find the most expensive and offensive outfit we could.

"You know, Molly," says Shaunna, reaching over and checking out my price tag (£495), "I think you should buy this suit for your weekend away with Dean. I could just see you strolling through the streets of Dublin wearing this!"

That should be funny, but I'm not laughing. Mainly because Ireland feels about as remote as Iceland for a holiday destination right now.

"Oh, Mol . . . you *still* haven't told your parents, have you?" Jude sighs, clocking my expression.

"Um . . . no."

70

Honestly, every time I've made a move to approach them, Mia pops up, or Dad nods off, or Mum's favourite movie comes on the telly, or I come up with yet another excuse to leave it till later. . .

"Omigod, Mol – your mum and dad don't *still* think you're coming on holiday with us, do they?"

Urgh, make me feel worse, why don't you, Shaunna. . .

"Well, *yeah*."

"But we could have really landed you in it! What if we'd phoned you up and got one of your parents? What if they'd spoken about you coming away with us on holiday and me or Jude had blurted out that it's not happening?"

Ah . . . good point. I'd never thought of that. I've been too busy with stuff like working up the courage to tell my mum and dad, bottling out, and working up the courage to tell Dean I'd bottled out.

"What's Dean saying?" asks Jude, speaking of the devil (not that he is – not in a million years).

"He's pretty cool about it, I suppose, but I think it's starting to bug him. He keeps saying it's not as if my parents are super-strict and will lock me in the cellar for the next ten years to keep me away from temptation or anything."

"*And* you'll be nearly seventeen by the time you go, so they can hardly complain," Jude points out. "I mean, it *is* legal, right?"

"Yeah, well, sex might be legal," Shaunna says to Jude's reflection in the mirror, "but it's not *compulsory*. You know, Mol, you don't *have* to go on this holiday if you feel weird about it. . ."

"It's not *that*!" I shake my head irritably, feeling my face flush so pink that I practically match Shaunna's hideous spangly frock and nails.

It's funny, for all the years the three of us giggled over the idea of sex, we've never spoken about it in terms of me and Dean, and Shaunna and Adam. Maybe it's because we all know each other too well, and that's what makes it weird. That's why I couldn't face talking to either of them about what happened That Night, and how messed up it had made me feel. But that's all sorted anyway. The timing wasn't right then; *that*'s why I felt so freaked out. In Dublin, it'll be right. It'll be *more* than right – it'll be perfect. . .

"Hey, don't get so worked up about telling your mum and dad, then! It's like Dean says, they're not exactly the type to flip out – not like mine!" says Shaunna, wrapping a comforting arm around my stuffed shoulders.

Doing that, the front of her spangly dress gapes

wider. Just as well she's wearing a bra, or it would be the exact boob-exposing pose tabloid photographers *dream* of snapping outside celeb-studded parties.

"It's just finding the right time to tell them."

"Come on – you're now the queen of all the spook stuff, Molly! Haven't you figured out the right time yet, by studying the ascension of the stars or the quadrants of the moon or something?"

"Yeah, yeah, yeah," I roll my eyes at Shaunna, spotting her sarcasm a mile off.

"No, honestly – what about all those coincidences you're always going on about? They're still happening, right?"

"Well," I shrug uncertainly, "I keep having that same recurring dream about the field and the rain, and every time I get it, we end up soaked at work the next day. . ."

"See? There you go!" Shaunna insists, not really noticing that that particular example of a coincidence wasn't exactly something to cheer about. "So come on, Mental Molly – why don't you use your spook powers to help yourself? And while you're at it, can you tell me and Jude some good news about *our* summer? What positive stuff do we need to do to stop us being bored out of our brains for the next six weeks, stuck in that sodding dullsville supermarket?"

Ooh. . . I feel a little surge of excitement. It's like my horoscope said – when it comes to friendships, I could be a bit surprised at the turn of events. Who'd have guessed that my mates would actually ask me for advice on something spiritual?

"So you're really fed-up, then?" I ask both their reflections.

Jude nods. Hard.

"Mol, it's only been a week and already I get *so* bored at work that there are days when I seriously consider gnawing my arm off, just for fun." Shaunna sighs theatrically.

"Well, you've got to follow your instincts . . . that's all *I've* been doing," I say. "And once you start doing that, you see which direction Fate is trying to point you in."

Even if that does seem to be a muddy field for me at the moment.

"You sound like one of those brochures from the alternative health fair the other day," Jude says, frowning at me.

"Yeah – do you fancy saying all that in English, and not hocus-pocus-ish?" Shaunna eyeballs me.

"It's like . . . well, it's like . . . I mean, what do you most feel like doing at the moment, Shaunna?" I fluster around for the right words.

How strange – we're having serious conversations

about sex (almost) and Fate (definitely), dressed up like we're extras out of some really corny sitcom set in suburbia.

"What, apart from the pleasure of handing this dress back to the snooty sales assistant and telling her I want to see something more expensive?"

"*Apart* from that, Shaun," I tell her.

"I'd guess I'd like. . ." Shaunna screws up her eyes, deep in thought. "I'd like to do something *radical*."

"Like?"

"Like. . . I dunno. Like learning to ride a boogie-board in the Great Barrier Reef, or . . . or driving through the Amazon rainforest in an open-top jeep, or sky-diving out of a plane into the Mojave desert, or learning to be a trapeze artist, or. . ."

"Whoa! That's *it*!"

"What's it?" Shaunna laughs at me. "Are you going to tell me you've got two tickets to the Great Barrier Reef in your backpack?"

"No," I shake my head and burble excitedly. "I'm trying to tell you that's *it* – *that's* what you should do! The trapeze thing, I mean! Didn't you see that big ad in the local paper on Saturday? About the courses the Arts Council's running this summer? I'm *sure* there was a one-day circus skills course in it!"

"Was there?" Shaunna's eyes light up. "*Seriously?*"

"Seriously! See what I mean about Fate pointing you in the right direction?"

"Yeah, yeah, whatever. Do you still have the newspaper?"

"Should do – as long as Mum hasn't chucked them out for recycling," I say, thrilled to see Shaunna so enthusiastic that her sequins are vibrating. "Hold on – I'll give Mum a quick call to check. . ."

I rustle over to my cubicle in the gawdy satin suit (close your eyes and it might sound as if you were inside a *bin*bag), and grab my phone out of my bag. But before I can dial, I see I have a text message.

Told M+D yet? Call U l8r – luv U, D xxx

I don't know why, but somehow I feel slightly irked reading that; like Dean's gatecrashed our girls' day out or something.

"Um, actually, I think she's out right now. I'll try her later," I say casually, as I chuck the phone back in my bag like it's suddenly infectious.

"What about me?" Jude gazes at me forlornly.

Jude has a tendency to come across like a stray spaniel sometimes; all pathetic, soppy eyes and in need of a decent meal, or a cuddle, or both. Only, dressed the way she is today, I guess the look is more stray leopard.

"Well, what do *you* want most at the moment?" I ask her.

"A boyfriend," she smiles sadly. "A nice one, preferably. I'm not fussy . . . just as long as he's got all the usual stuff – two eyes, a nose, an arm or two. That sort of thing."

"Jude, you wouldn't recognize a nice guy if he came up to you in the street with a neon sign taped to his body saying 'Nice guy'!" giggles Shaunna. "Your radar only picks up trouble!"

It's true. Jude's track record would not make a great basis for a romantic novel. Sweet as she is, she has the worst possible taste in blokes. If you're male and happen to be a liar, scumbag, bully or git in general, you have an excellent chance of having Jude Conrad fall flat on her face in love with you.

Which presents a problem. How do we get Jude together with a nice guy? Where is Fate storing this special person who's going to change our buddy's run of bad luck in the boy department?

"Any nice lads at work?" I suggest.

Vaguely, I'm aware of Jude shaking her head, but what I'm *really* listening to is my brain rattling an amazing thought through my head.

77

Of *course* there's a nice lad at work. But he works alongside *me*, not Jude and Shaunna. He's funny and thoughtful; he tries to act like a knight in shining armour and pull you out of the path of danger (or at least the path of engulfing sprays of mud), only I didn't realize that straight away, did I, because I was too busy being such a hard-hearted cynic that first day I met Cameron.

"Jude," I grin. "I think I might just know the very person for you. . .!"

"*Yessss!*" Shaunna yelps, holding her palm out towards Jude for a high-five.

In her excitement, Jude slaps harder than she means to, but I'm sure that Shaunna is so pleased at the idea of Jude potentially dating a non-git that she doesn't even seem to mind that the nail on her index finger is now somersaulting through the air – and straight towards the nosey nose of the snooty shop assistant, who's come to spy on us.

"Excuse me, but this outfit is tat," Shaunna addresses the woman, without missing a beat. "Do you have anything similar, only not so cheap?"

Me and Jude dive for our cubicles and our real clothes, practically exploding with suppressed giggles and desperately hoping we can get dressed and make our escape before Shaunna gets us physically *chucked* out. . .

chapter eight
Splat.

Date: *Tuesday 30th July*

Frame of mind: *Guilty*

Twists of Fate: *Twist of a leg, more like...*

I *am* destined to have a good summer. . . I *am* destined to have a good summer. . . I *am* destined to have a good summer. . .

I've got to keep that in my head. I need to dig out that old horoscope if I've still got it somewhere and re-read it till I believe it.

What exactly was Adam Pindar's little gem of wisdom again? You know, the stuff Shaunna was telling me last week in the changing room at Partington's – just before the store manageress came and asked us to please leave. . . Oh yeah – *act* confident and everyone will *think* you're confident. Well, with every step along this grey-floored corridor tonight, I'm trying to think myself positive, so that everyone – including me – gets fooled into assuming that that's how I feel.

What a joke.

You try and come across all cheerful when you're about to visit a best mate who's in hospital with suspected cracked tibias, fibulas and God knows what else, after a tumble off a trapeze. A best friend whose broken bits and bones are all *your* fault. A best friend who'd never have done a circus skills course unless *you'd* suggested the stupid thing in the first place.

Oh, the guilt. . .

"Excuse me," I say to a harassed-looking nurse, who scuttles past me like I'm invisible. Or maybe it's just that my *voice* is invisible. I'm feeling so bad that I'm talking in a small helium squeak. I have been ever since Dad called me to the phone an hour ago and passed me on to Shaunna's panic-stricken mother.

Urgh. . . I'm going to have to face not only Shaunna (unrecognizable in swathes of bandages,

 80

no doubt), but also her parents, who will probably want to *stone* me for harming a long, curly hair on their precious daughter's head. And I couldn't blame them.

But first I have to find where exactly the hospital has stashed my battered and bruised best friend. And to do that, I've got to find my voice *and* find a nurse who is willing to acknowledge my existence.

"Erm, hello. . ." I say to a crop-haired, dark-skinned boy who looks about twelve, but who *is* wearing some kind of blue hospital-type outfit.

OK, so he's more eighteen than twelve when he looks up from the trolley of cardboard cowboy hats he's mysteriously pushing in front of him, but it's hard to tell when you're hiding behind a large bunch of chrysanthemums. (Me – not him.)

"You need help?" he asks.

Do *you*? I feel like asking back, wondering what's with the cardboard cowboy hats.

"Yes, I'm trying to find my friend, Shaunna – Shaunna Sullivan," I explain, feeling my nose twitching with pollen. "She just came in here a couple of hours ago."

"Shaunna Sullivan," mutters the boy, leaving his trolley and going to inspect a scribbled-on whiteboard on a nearby wall. "Oh, here she is. . .

Bed four. It's just that side ward at the very end of this corridor."

"Marcus!" a female voice calls out from the other end of the corridor and grabs the boy's attention. "Can you hurry up, please? We really need those sample containers in toilet three!"

"Got to go!" smiles the boy, tapping the cowboy hats. "Hope your friend is OK!"

"Um, thanks."

I hide a grimace behind the chrysanthemums. *Yuck.* The hats – they're pee-catchers! What have I done? I'm responsible not only for causing untold physical damage to Shaunna, but because of me, she has to wee in a cardboard bucket. . .

"About time!" a loud voice echoes down the corridor.

Good grief – it's Shaunna, looking like . . . Shaunna.

"Shouldn't you be lying down?!" I ask, hurrying towards her.

Not to mention plastered up, I think to myself.

"Yeah, but I got bored," yawns Shaunna, leading the way back to her ruffled bed. "I was heading for the TV lounge just to pass the time. Hope you brought chocolates. There's no point me being here if I'm not going to get spoiled. . ."

"But how are you?"

I plonk myself at the edge of her bed and place the flowers on the moveable meal tray (currently weighed down with magazines).

"Fine!" Shaunna shrugs, scratching her head through her mop of long, wavy hair. "Bit of a headache, that's all. But serves me right for landing on it, I suppose!"

"But I thought you'd broken something!"

Running my eyes over her, I do a quick count of body parts (all intact, by the look of it).

"Oh, God! You've been speaking to my mother of course, haven't you? The woman for whom the phrase 'Drama Queen' was invented!"

"Um, yes. But she did sound very upset. . ."

"Mol, doctors had to *sedate* her when she took me and my sister Ruth for our jabs when we were babies. She got hysterical!" says Shaunna, flopping back on her pillows, arms behind her head. "It was like today – OK, so they had to X-ray me for safety's sake, just to check I hadn't snapped anything important, but the way *she* was going on, you'd think they were doing open-heart surgery on me. Dad had to restrain her from calling every living relative to my bedside for a fond farewell. . ."

"But you are all right . . . aren't you?" I double-check.

"More or less – they just want me to stay in overnight for observation, since I *might* have concussion."

"So where's your mum now?" I ask tentatively, half-expecting to be swept aside by a wailing mother at any second.

"I managed to get rid of her for a while by asking her to go home with Dad and collect some pyjamas and a toothbrush for me. Thought it would buy me some time to see you guys and Adam without her hanging around, mopping my fevered brow. . ."

"Hey, no one gets to mop bits of you except me!" says Adam, breezing into the ward with a giant inflatable Tigger balloon and a six-pack of Quavers.

"Brilliant!" Shaunna cries out, tearing open the bag.

I notice that a week's worth of table-clearing and a day's worth of falling off trapezes have taken their toll on the last of her fake nails. Instead of long, lustrous and plain loopy, they're back to short and bitten, with chipped purple varnish that I've just noticed matches the bruise that's showing under her fringe. Shaunna . . . she's nothing if not colour co-ordinated.

"Hey, listen, Molly," says Adam, fixing me with a hard stare, "next time you suggest my girlfriend takes up a new hobby, can you make sure it's cro-cheting doilies, or patting puppies, or rolling in cushions or something safe? It's just that she hasn't got many brain cells as it is—"

"Oi!" barks an indignant Shaunna, battering him with the six-pack of crisps.

"—and she can't afford to lose any more!" Adam grins wickedly, grabbing the rustling sack of Quavers away from her. "Now see? Playing 'Catch' with crisps! *That's* a nice safe hobby to have!"

Just as they start play-fighting for possession of the Quavers, I spot Jude worriedly peeking into the ward.

"Come in!" I wave her over.

"Aren't you only supposed to be allowed two people in at a time?" she asks warily, glancing around at the other three patients in the room and their token pairs of visitors.

"Two people in a bed at one time?" says Adam, pulling back the sheet and wriggling in beside Shaunna. "Nah! There's plenty of room if you and Molly don't mind getting in at the bottom end. Hey, I know! Let's ask some of the other patients to join in! We could go for a record: how many sick people can you get in a hospital bed!"

"*You're* sick, Adam Pindar," Shaunna shakes her head ruefully, but still budges up to make room for him. "Anyway, don't worry about the visitor thing, Jude; I'm expecting my mum back in a little while and for some unknown reason she's planning on dragging my dad, my gran, my sister and her husband along with her."

"Think of the gifts!"

That's typical Adam-talk. I'm almost smiling, but it's wavering as I check out Adam and Shaunna fooling around and snuggling under the sheets together. I wonder, have they ever. . .?

"But how are you, Shaunnie? Your mum made it sound as if you'd be in traction till you were thirty-five!" Jude comments, as she drags a spare chair over to Shaunna's bedside.

"Jude, you should *know* my mother by now. She watches too many hospital dramas. Whatever she tells you, divide it by five and take it with a pinch of salt, and that's more like the truth."

"So what *is* wrong with you?" Jude frowns. "You look pretty healthy to me. Are you sure this isn't a way to skive a couple of days off work?"

"Concussion," Shaunna explains, holding up her fringe to show off the bruise.

"Eyeshadow," Adam whispers behind his hand in the direction of me and Jude. "She probably put it on just before we arrived to get us feeling sorry for her. . ."

"But what did you actually *do*, Shaun?"

As Jude asks this question, she slaps her hand over Adam's mouth. Which is fair enough, really.

"I came off the trapeze and did a perfect landing – on my head," says Shaunna, matter-of-factly. "We'd had a long lecture from the trainer about how to dismount properly, but I was too busy checking out her fancy costume and didn't listen. It's my own fault."

"It's *my* fault!" I blurt out in Shaunna's direction, ending my guilt-ridden silence while the others fooled around.

"It is *not* your fault, Mol! It was a *good* idea to go to the circus skills thing! It's not your fault that I have the attention span of a flea!"

"Lucky you've got a head of concrete," mutters Adam, planting a quick kiss on Shaunna's bruise.

"I tell you what *is* your fault, though, Molly," Jude grins at me, settling back in her chair and folding her skinny arms across her chest.

"What?" I panic, ignoring her grin.

"It's *your* fault that I went on the *lousiest* date of my life last night!"

"You mean. . ." I say, the truth dawning on me.

"Yep, your so-called friend, Cameron," Jude announces. "He called me last night, and we went out for a pizza."

I had no idea; I hadn't seen him since Sunday.
We didn't have any *mmm . . . milk* work on yesterday or today.

"*And?*" Shaunna beams, bouncing up and down on the bed like a kid on Christmas morning.

"And you didn't *like* him?" I frown, thinking of ever-smiling, ever-joking Cameron, who'd seemed so sweetly taken aback when I told him at the Stourwood Horse Show last week that I thought he and Jude might get on really well.

"*Like* him?" Jude snorts. "He was a creep!"

"Yeah, but that's the type you usually go for, isn't it, Jude?" Shaunna butts in mischievously.

"He was always *touching* me," Jude shudders.

"Oo-er – isn't there a law against that?"

That's Adam. Again. Obviously.

"On the *arm*, Adam, or round the *waist*," Jude stresses, before Adam makes it any worse. "It was just really . . . yucky."

"But that's just the way he is!" I try to stand up for Cameron. "He's just . . . *friendly* that way. He doesn't mean anything by it!"

Jude raises her eyebrows at that – she's not buying my explanation at all.

"But you know why he *really* messed up the date?" she leans forward to ask me.

"Was it the point when he asked you to go nude

88

roller-blading with him?" Adam suggests from the sidelines, before Shaunna whacks him over the head with her crisps again.

I shake my head at Jude.

"It was because he spent the entire time talking about this other girl who he was obviously *totally* in love with. Which wasn't very flattering for me."

"Oooh, *bad* move. That is *so* not the way to impress a date," Adam chips in again. (He just can't help himself.)

"Really?" asks Shaunna, now wrapping both her hands around her boyfriend's mouth. "Who's the lucky girl that octopus boy is lusting after, then?"

Jude blinks her big, brown eyes at me and says nothing.

"No *way*!" giggles Shaunna, turning to stare at me too. . .

Oh, the relief to be away from that ward and out here in the fresh, cool air.

When you're being ganged up on by three people who are all considerably louder than you at the best of times, the only thing you can do is retreat as gracefully as you can.

And *fume*.

God, it is *so* maddening when people won't listen to you. Of *course* Cameron doesn't fancy me! We *work* together, and Jude is one of my best friends. Until they got to know each other better (fat chance of *that* now), the only thing they had in common was me, so no wonder I came up in the conversation a few times.

I know Jude's problem – it's that whole thing about her only going for bad boys. . . One whiff of a truly nice guy and straight away she's trying to find fault in him. I don't know why I bothered to set up that stupid blind date at all. What am I meant to say to Cameron when I see him at work tomorrow?

And while I'm going into fretting overload, how did I manage to screw up so badly when it came to helping Shaunna and Jude out? How did I get the fate signals so wrong?

Urgh. . . I feel terrible. I need someone to tell me I'm not a walking disaster who messes with my mates' lives. I need kind words and a large hug, and I need them now.

I check my watch: Dean should be almost finished his shift at the lido. If I phone him, we could meet up halfway, at the—

The chimes of the *Bagpuss* theme tune make me jump. Grabbing my mobile, I smile at the display – it's the first happy coincidence I've had in days.

"Dean! I was just going to call you!" I beam at him down the phone.

"Yeah? How's Shaunna! I just picked up your text. . ."

"She's fine – I just left her a couple of minutes ago. I'll tell you all about it later; do you fancy meeting up?" I find myself raising my voice, as a cackle of loud laughter rings out at Dean's end of the airwaves.

"Did you say meet up? Sorry, Mol – I can't. That's what I was calling to tell you; we just found out it's Stevie's birthday, and all the lifeguard crew are going out to celebrate."

Stevie? I can't figure out who that is . . . I haven't met anyone that Dean is working with yet, but I don't remember him talking about any lad called Stevie. . .

"Stevie. . .?" I frown into the receiver.

"C'mon, Deano! Get a move on!" I hear a girl's voice giggle somewhere very close to Dean's phone.

"OK, OK, Stevie! Get off!" Dean is obviously grinning at this point. "Sorry, Mol – better go!"

"Stephanie!" cackles another – male – voice. "Put that boy down! You don't know where he's been!"

"Call you tomorrow, yeah?"

"OK," I hear my helium voice squeak, as I try and figure out why I've never heard Dean mention a Stephanie in connection with work either. A Stephanie – aka Stevie – who seems *more* than comfortable to give my boyfriend a bearhug, by the sounds of it.

I'm not sure if humans are supposed to have hackles but I'm pretty sure I can feel mine rising. . .

chapter nine

Take a deep breath and...

Date: *Wednesday 31st July*

Frame of mind: *Wobbly*

Twists of Fate: *Too wound-up to spot any*

Reasons I fell in love with Dean:

1) He was so sweet to Shaunna when they first went out. Watching them together last summer, I kept thinking, I wish someone adored *me* that way.

2) Knowing that Shaunna was still fantasizing about Star-Boy (i.e. the waste-of-space mystery man she spent a year drooling over till she realized he was a prize git), it broke my heart to see Dean

being rejected. That's when I knew how much he mattered to me.

3) Feeling like my heart was being pulverized with marshmallow hammers every time he spoke to me (while he was still going out with Shaunna; while she was *still* lusting after her Star-Boy).

4) The crinkles on his nose, every time he smiled. (*Especially* when that smile was aimed at me!)

5) The day he said yes, when I asked him out (the only time I've EVER asked a boy out).

6) The first time we kissed, when I thought I'd faint/giggle/turn to mush I was so happy.

Reasons I love Dean now:
1) Because. . .

OK, I'll come back to that later. There's too many distractions going on right now. One of them being my kid sister.

"Urgh! They look like they're a hundred years old!" sniggers Mia, pointing at the brown-tinged, once white trainers that I've just tried to scrub clean for the millionth time this week.

"So would *you* if you'd rolled around in a vat of mud for a fortnight!" I tug at one of Mia's long blonde plaits as she pads out of the kitchen with the Petits Filous she's just nabbed from the fridge.

"Hey, remember *Austin Powers 2*?" Dean mumbles from the breakfast bar, through a mouthful of toasted-cheese sandwich he's just helped himself to. Life-saving seems to be giving him an appetite.

"What about it?" I ask, stuffing my hated white jeans and T-shirt into the washer-dryer, so they'll be ready in time for tomorrow's mud-fest. (Told you I had distractions.)

"Dr Evil in the movie – he had a Mini-Me clone. Remember?"

"Um, I suppose. . ." I frown, wondering if Dean's brain has been affected in any way by excessive exposure to chlorine. Or maybe he's still on a high after the great night out he had last night with all his new chums from work. . .

"Well, look at Mia!" says Dean, with a pretty unattractive dollop of pickle stuck to the corner of his mouth. "She's your double with those plaits! She's your Mini-Me! No, wait . . . she's your Mini-Mia!"

Any other time I might have laughed at that (hey, that's what love makes you do – laugh at each other's jokes, however lame they are), but I'm not in the mood right now. Today's not been a great day on the planet: for a start, there was the whole, awkward thing with Cameron, where he inevitably brought up the disastrous date with Jude ("Sorry, Mol – I don't really think me and Jude hit it off. . ."); then there was the usual daily downpour and muddy field to navigate; *then* there was the fact that I was *actually* travel sick (as opposed to just *feeling* travel sick) when Danielle touched warp factor nine on the way back to town in the Milk Mobile this afternoon.

And that's not even *starting* on the nagging worries I've been having about the someone called Stevie. . .

"Psst!" hisses Dean, clocking that Mia is safely out of earshot. "Have you told them yet?"

He has to bring *that* up again, doesn't he? Could my day be any more hideous?

"No," I snap, rattling too much washing powder into the fill-tray.

"Well, don't you think you should? It's only a month away," I hear Dean whisper. "OK, I'm not exactly expecting them to get the champagne out and tell us how delighted they are about it, but your mum and dad have got to know! And so do I – I got a phone call from the hotel in Dublin today; they want to know if I'm confirming the provisional booking. . ."

The hotel – omigod.

 96

The whole thing had sounded so romantic and beautiful when Dean had first suggested it. A renovated Georgian house a stone's throw from the river; the bustle of friendly people who don't know or care who we are as we stroll hand-in-hand through the cobbled streets, back to our room with the four-poster bed. . .

But that was then and this is now, and all I can picture is some stuffy, staid hotel manned by disapproving adults who will take *one* look at sixteen-going-on-seventeen me and seventeen-going-on-eighteen Dean, and think exactly *one* thought: dirty weekend. (And they'd be right. . .)

I can feel my face flushing now, and wish I hadn't tied up my hair in those stubby plaits today – I want to screen my blushes, even from Dean. They make me feel such a complete *kid*.

"Mol? What do you think? You're really quiet!"

"I think it's fine!" I say snappily, knowing I sound irritable, but not sure how to stop it.

"So?"

"*So?*" I repeat, with an edge to my voice I hadn't expected to be there.

"So, what will we do about it?"

Dean sounds calm and infuriatingly rational about it all, like it's so easy to tell your parents that you're . . . well, that you're basically planning to have *sex*.

Oh, I feel sick. . .

"So, it sounds like you had a good time with Stevie and everyone last night," I say, changing the subject clumsily.

Not that Dean seems to notice.

"Yeah!" he laughs, wiping the grease from his mouth with the back of his hand and then rubbing his hand on the thigh of his jeans. Yuck. "Stevie's something else! You should have heard the stuff she was saying to the waiters in Pizza Hut. God, we were all *cringing* for the poor blokes! She's just totally upfront; totally up for anything!"

Is she really?

I feel a cold shiver slither down my backbone, and pretend to fiddle with the lid of the fabric conditioner, just to hide my discomfort. Doesn't he understand that I don't want to hear about how great this girl is? Doesn't he realize—

"Mol*leeeee*! *Deannnn!*" I hear my mum call through from the living room. "Come through here, you two – you've got to see what's on the telly!"

I speed through without a backward glance, only aware that Dean's following when his bigger feet thud behind, just out of step with mine.

"What's up?" I fix a smile on my face, and gaze unconcerned at the TV screen, which just happens to be showing a pretty picture of a seaside town somewhere.

"That's where you're going, isn't it?" Mum beams, her arms wrapped round Mia on the sofa, but still managing to point.

I don't know what she's on about. Is it some local news programme highlighting the soggiest county fairs planned this week?

"It's the *Holiday Show*," Dad tries to explain, lazily scratching his beard as he nods his head towards the telly. "That's the resort you and the girls are going to, isn't it?"

"And look!" squeals Mia. "Caravans! Are they the ones you're going to be staying in, Molly?"

My heart starts sinking, but is jerked to a standstill on its downward journey by the dig in the ribs I get courtesy of Dean's elbow. Right now, I'd like nothing more than for there to be a freak earthquake that swallows me up whole. But knowing the weather round our way, the only meteorological catastrophe that's likely to strike is a mudslide . . . and chances are *that's* not going to happen in the next ten minutes in my very own lounge.

"Mum. . . Dad. . ."

Gulp. I'm talking in my tiny, helium voice, but somehow – after years of practice – my parents still tune in to it.

"Yes, honey?" Mum smiles broadly, while twiddling one of Mia's plaits.

"I'm not going on holiday with Jude and Shaunna any more."

There.

I've said it.

It can't get any worse.

"What?" Dad frowns. "You girls haven't fallen out, have you?"

Urgh. . . I forgot about the other bit.

"No. It's just. . . It's just . . . uhhh. . ."

"It's just that me and Molly are going on holiday together instead. We're going away for a long weekend in Dublin," I hear Dean boom, and feel myself cringe inside, even though his arms are now supportively weaving their way around me.

"You're *what*?!" bellows Dad.

Uh-oh . . . that doesn't sound too good.

"Mia – go upstairs and get ready for bed now, please," Mum snaps at my sister.

"But Mum, it's only half-past—"

"Mia! *Now*, please!" Mum barks sternly.

Double uh-oh, if there is such a thing. . .

chapter ten

Don't I know you from somewhere...?

Date: *Monday 5th August*

Frame of mind: *Fried*

Twists of Fate: *You really don't want to know*

What exactly had my parents said?

Oh, yeah ... they'd always *trusted* me. They were *disappointed* in me. In fact, they were very, very *upset*. They thought I had more *sense*. They thought they could trust Dean, and they thought *he* had more sense, not to mention respect (that was *after* they'd asked him to leave).

Oh, yes, it had been fun and games in my house

the night we'd let Mum and Dad in on our romantic, idyllic, warms-the-cockles-of-your-heart plans to celebrate our first anniversary.

You'd think we'd told them that we'd wanted to set up an animal-testing lab, the way my parents reacted. I tell you, if I'd told them I planned to start up an endangered tiger-hunting expedition for rich, arrogant businessmen in a gap year between school and university, I think they'd have been happier than they were with the news me and Dean sprung on them.

"*Wheeeee!*"

"Dean! Put her down! She'll be sick!"

In fact, *I* feel sick, just *watching* Dean hold Mia under the arms and spin her around and around in her clashing pink T-shirt and spotty-dotty, lime-green and orange shorts.

"She's fine!" Dean insists, though he slows down and deposits my sister back on *terra firma*.

His arms are very tanned, I notice. Brown as a berry, as the saying goes – though I can't actually think of any berries that are brown. . .

"I'm all right!" Mia insists, steadying herself against Dean as her sense of balance struggles to reassert itself.

It's the contrast of Mia's pale skin against Dean's that makes him look all the more sun-kissed. How come the sun seems to shine happily in the vicinity of the local lido, but the rain clouds gather over practically every out-of-town venue *I* have to work at?

"Look, I just want us to have a nice time, and I don't want Mia being sick, OK?" I tell Dean. "It was bad enough her feeling ill in the car out here."

"Here" is the zoo, a day out dreamt up by me and Dean as a treat for my kid sister. OK, as a nice gesture that we figured might just get us back in my parents' good books after the fireworks of last week. . .

"But I *didn't* feel sick in Dean's car!" Mia insists. "I only asked if we could open the window!"

"Yeah, and I wasn't driving fast, Mol!" says Dean, a little chastised. "You know what I'm like with my dad's car – I'm too paranoid I'll bump it to do anything stupid!"

I *know* that, I *know* that, I *know* that. . . I guess I'm just a bit paranoid myself right now; every time I get in the Milk Mobile I'm filled with dread that Danielle's maniacal rally-driving style is going to make me barf all over my nice white *Mmm . . . Milk!* T-shirt, or get us involved in yet another near-collision with random cars, lorries, buses and cows. (Oh, yes – we had a close call on Saturday when Danielle nearly reversed into the newly proclaimed

Show Champion Aberdeen Angus, all because she was too busy checking in the rear-view mirror for smudges of lipstick on her teeth.)

"Can I have an ice-cream, please, Molly?" Mia suddenly bursts out, spying a stray ice-cream vendor strolling into our line of vision with his refrigerated cart.

It's a meltingly hot day, and I wouldn't mind something cold myself, but I don't want to encourage Mia – apart from a burger and chips at lunchtime she's already eaten her body-weight in popcorn, Rolos, candy-floss and wine gums. If she has anything else with sugar in, I might as well take her to the dentist on the way home.

"No, you've had enough, Mia," I shake my head.

"Aw, come on, Mol! We're having a day out! Let her have an ice-cream!"

Mia turns and beams up at her favourite bloke in the whole wide world. She has a terrible crush on Dean, she really does. It was the *Star Trek* thing that really did it for her. When she discovered that Dean was a sci-fi buff with a particular soft spot for her own number one telly show, she was sold. And when he bought her a *Star Trek* suit for her last birthday, he had a fan for life.

"It's just that. . ."

I trail off when I spot Dean doing the old pulling-a-coin-out-of-your ear trick.

"Wow! Look at that!" he gasps, staring at the pound coin that's just magicked its way out of the side of my sister's head.

He tosses it upwards with a grin, letting Mia catch it in mid-air, before she yelps a "Thank you, Dean!" and makes a run for the ice-cream cart.

"*Dean!*" I sigh with exasperation.

"What?" my boyfriend laughs back at me, a look of roguish innocence on his face. "I thought we were meant to be having fun today, weren't we? Isn't that what you're meant to do at the zoo?"

"Yes," I nod wearily. "It's just that I'd kind of prefer it if she spent more time looking at the animals than working out what she's going to stuff her face with next!"

"Ooh, you're going to make *such* a strict mum!" Dean teases, walking towards me with his arms outstretched.

I duck away from Dean and his oncoming arms and start walking towards Mia. I didn't really appreciate that joke – I'm sixteen, and don't want to come over all mumsy and sensible. And I don't really like to be reminded of the word "Mum" either, not with the strange atmosphere there's been at home all week. Normally, I get on with my parents so well and I hate sensing that they're hugely disappointed in me. And I particularly hated that conversation I had with Mum the day after me and Dean had hit them with the holiday news.

Honestly, you don't know the *meaning* of the word mortifying unless you've sat through a conversation as cringesome and awful as that. I mean, my mum only goes and asks straight out if me and Dean are already sleeping together. My God! Of *course* we're not, but we might as *well* be. The night before, she and Dad made me feel like some slaggy strumpet for wanting to go away for one measly weekend to Ireland with my boyfriend of a whole year, and now here she was asking me the most personal, embarrassing question ever! How would *she* like it if I asked how often she and Dad . . . urgh, I don't even want to *go* there. . .

"Meet you in the petting zoo!" Mia calls out, zooming off with her ice-cream as fast as her daisy-decorated sandals will carry her.

"Dean – you can't just give in to what other people want all the time!" I turn around and bark at him.

Dean's face darkens.

"Whoa! What's this all about? Ever since I picked you guys up, you've had a face on you!"

 106

"No I haven't!" I argue back, only angered more by the confusion in Dean's face.

God . . . what am I *doing* with this person? OK, we never talked about it, but doesn't he have the faintest, *tiniest* idea what I've been upset about recently?

My head's held low, my mind swamped in sudden misery.

And then a strong hand slithers into mine . . . and I *melt*. Here comes that semi-forgotten, soothing sense of comfort – a sense that whatever's stressing me out, I can just lean my head on Dean's broad chest and he can make it all better.

I turn and find myself smiling at his kind, handsome face, and watch as the smile he beams back at me makes the freckles on his nose disappear into that familiar cute maze of crinkles.

"You all right?" he says softly, giving my hand a squeeze.

"Kind of," I shrug.

"*Is* it me? Have I done something wrong?"

"No."

"It'll all work out, Mol. Your parents will come round, once they get used to the idea of us going away together. They just need time."

I want to believe him, I really do.

"C'mere," Dean whispers, leaning towards me

and cupping his hand gently around my neck as he pulls me close for a kiss.

Oh, Dean. . . I whisper in my head as I feel the familiar soft warmth of his mouth on mine. A tight ball of tension that I didn't even know was there starts unfurling in my stomach and I'm more relaxed in this moment than I've been in who-knows-how-long. . .

Dean begins to slide his hand from my neck on to my shoulder, and with that small movement, there's an unexpectedly tight tugging sensation at my throat, followed by a ping! and then a sudden slackness.

"My locket!" I whisper, breaking away from Dean and slapping a hand across my bare neck.

"Oh, jeez . . . it must've caught on my watch!" says Dean, holding up his wrist and staring dumbly at the short, broken piece of gold chain dangling from it.

"My heart!" I call out, falling on my knees and peering at the tarmac path for any sign of the broken necklace. "I've got to find it! Gran gave it to me!"

"Calm down, Mol!" Dean frowns, bending down and joining in the search. "It's not like it was expensive – and your gran's so forgetful she probably doesn't even remember giving it to you. I can always buy you another one if we can't find it. . ."

Out of the blue, a wave of silent tears rushes from somewhere in the middle of my chest and streams down my face. Dean hasn't noticed yet; he's too busy scouring the ridged ground for my little gold heart. This is crazy; I don't even know why I'm crying. Yes, I do – it's sadness . . . the sadness of knowing that my head is swirling and I can't rest it on Dean's head and rely on him to make everything better. Mainly because *he's* part of the problem. *He's* the one who's helped put this big wedge of weirdness between me and my parents. And *he's* the one who has a friend called Stevie who he suddenly hasn't been able to shut up about for the last week or so (it's been all "Me and Stevie" *this*, "Me and Stevie" *that*). Honestly, it's really starting to do my head in. . .

"Shit!"

Dean's yelp startles me out of my misery, and for a millisecond I can't figure out what's made him leap to his feet in alarm. And then I hear it – the faraway high-pitched wailing of my little sister. . .

It wasn't the goat's fault.

If *I'd* just been kicked in the hind leg by a brattish five-year-old thug, I think I might have automatically bitten the nearest finger waggling in my face too.

"Are you OK?" I check with Mia for the millionth time.

She nods silently, swinging her legs back and forth on the plastic hospital chair, her injured finger resting in her lap like a bandaged baby bird.

"Want a Coke?" I ask, ferreting around in my pocket for change for the vending machine I'd just spotted on the other side of the packed waiting room.

Mia nods again, her big blue eyes looking abnormally huge and round against her miserably pale, gaunt face.

Hmm.

I don't think it's just the goat bite that's upset her, or the fuss at the zoo's First Aid room when the nurse told her she might need a stitch and that we should get her finger properly checked out just in case. I think it's more to do with the row me and Dean had in the car on the way here.

I know he was only trying to help, but my nerves were so jangled that when Dean came out with the stuff about what a brilliant First Aider Stevie was and the amazing rescue she'd done during the week on some kid that had bumped his head on the bottom of the pool, I just flipped out.

"What's Stevie got to do with anything?" I'd barked. "Are you saying we should go down to the lido instead of Casualty? Do you think Stevie knows *more* about this kind of thing than a doctor?!"

It was feeble and it was pathetic. So was the bit where I stopped talking to him, *and* the bit where I told him to drop us at the hospital and go – we'd manage on our own.

"Urgh. . ." I wince, feeling my insides curling up with shame as the coins clunk into the machine and the can of Coke comes tumbling out.

I'm messing things up; I'm making them more complicated than they are . . . and I don't know why I'm doing it. Maybe it's because I feel like everything's somehow *unravelling*.

"There you go!" I say brightly, snapping the ring-pull back and handing the can to Mia.

"Thank you," she mumbles softly, glancing at the collection of glum-faced people around us.

"Hey, let's play a game!" I nudge my sister, in an effort to cheer her up, even if I can't cheer myself up.

"What kind of game?" she narrows her eyes at me.

"The 'What's Wrong With Them?' game!" I announce.

"How does it work?" she frowns, in-between slurps of fizzy stuff.

"Well," I reply, lowering my voice and leaning conspiratorially close to her ear, "see that balding guy pacing around over there?"

She nods, registering the bland, middle-aged bloke striding back and forth at the far end of the room.

"*I* think he's here because he's got this humongous killer zit on his bum – that's the reason he's not sitting down!"

If you want a short cut to making a ten year old laugh, then coming out with the word "bum" usually does the trick. And dumb as it was, what I said has got Mia giggling her head off. Result.

Then again. . .

Mia's giggles have vanished as quickly as they came and she is now looking distinctly pea-green.

"Oh, no. . ." I mutter, "you're not going to be sick, are you, Mee?"

It's déjà vu. It's a coincidence of the barfing kind. And it's going to happen any second now and all I can do is stare around like a lunatic trying to figure out what I can do.

At the precise second that my sister loses control of the collision of Coke, candy-floss, wine gums etc. in her stomach, a large cardboard cowboy hat shoots under her chin, saving the tiled floor from imminent splattage.

"Very handy things, these," smiles someone I vaguely recognize.

"Thank you – thank you so much," I say to the boy in the blue cotton uniform, as I hold Mia's hair away from her face and rub her back comfortingly.

He smiles and shrugs, still holding the cardboard hat in a strategic, puke-catching position.

I fleetingly gaze at him again, and I suss where I've seen him before. "You. . . I thought you worked in the wards upstairs?"

That was the last time I'd seen – what had the nurse shouted? Oh yes, *Marcus* – it was when I was on my way to visit Shaunna after her flying (and falling) trapeze incident. He'd given me directions to her bed.

"I go wherever there are floors to be polished, samples to be collected, or toilets to clean!" he jokes bluntly.

"Like a superhero!" Mia whispers, recovering herself slightly.

"Dunno about that! Here let me get you something to wipe your mouth. . ." Marcus smiles, reaching over to grab a bundle of green paper towels from his trolley.

It's as he stretches that I notice the simple black tattoo on the dark brown skin of his bicep.

A heart.

Is that a coincidence or what? I think, reaching up to touch the locket that isn't there any more.

And what's with all the hairs standing up on the back of my neck. . .?

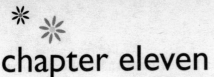

chapter eleven
Caught in a so-called snog

Date: *Tuesday 6th August*

Frame of mind: *Constantly alarmed*

Twists of Fate: *One of a lip-smacking, stomach-churning kind*

Last night, I lit a lavender-scented candle in my room and tried to meditate.

I think the point of meditation is that you're supposed to clear your mind, and that by clearing your mind, you clear out a lot of junk that's cluttering it up and stopping you from being happy. Stuff like guilt and worry and stress (it says on the label on the base of the candle).

That's all very well, but I bet the makers of that meditation candle have never worried about the bucketloads of guilt, worry and stress that *I* have. Try stepping in my size 39s and they may want to make themselves a bigger candle. . .

One thing was for sure – all that quiet, personal time I had to myself when I was meditating? It definitely gave me lots of time to mull over everything and come up with a simple conclusion: that *nothing* was going right in my life.

My room smelled really nice, though. . .

But that was then, this is now. I woke up this morning, determined to have a more positive outlook on the day, even if I did have to wear a T-shirt that had *Mmm . . . Milk!* printed across it.

My resolve to be more positive lasted for exactly three hours and forty-five minutes. It was the sight of the "See Into Your Future" stall that changed everything. More specifically, the sight of a familiar beige cardie (and the woman wearing it) – that's what tipped me over the edge into sorry-for-myself gloomsville.

Course, the mud-ball between the shoulder blades didn't help.

"Molly, what's up?" I hear Cameron's voice call out from the brolly-carrying, kagoul-wearing crowds.

I didn't think anyone would spot me here, huddled up miserably on the steps of the out-of-order portable loos. (Oh, the glamour! Will it never start!)

"Nothing!" I lie, parping my nose loudly into a scrunched paper tissue.

"It's got to be *some*thing!" says Cameron, nudging himself right up next to me on the narrow (and frankly cold) metal step.

He slips his arm around my shoulders, then immediately tugs it away.

"What's this?"

Cameron examines his newly-brown forearm.

"A mud-ball. . ." I mumble miserably.

"A *mud*-ball?" Cameron frowns through his sweet little specs. This close up, he actually reminds me of a blond Harry Potter. Only not twelve. And not a wizard.

"It's like a snowball, made of mud. A bunch of kids have been following me round, using me as target practice."

Even though it must be a gloopy and fairly unpleasant sensation, Cameron once again slides his arm around my back. What a gent.

The fact is, he's too nice to hang out with someone as horrible as me. After all, I am the guilt-ridden monster who let my ten-year-old sister get mutilated by a goat (thankfully no stitches needed), just 'cause I was too busy obsessing about other stuff, like plotting to go on holiday behind my parents' back with my boyfriend who I'm not even sure I'm going *out* with any more (since he didn't call me yesterday after the goat incident – and no wonder, since I'd been so ratty to him).

And then there's the guilt I feel for not phoning *him*, but that was because I felt guilty for having an instantaneous crush on the boy in the blue cotton uniform at the hospital, all because he was kind to my little sister and had an intriguing tattoo. In fact, up till a couple of minutes ago, I'd been doodling a traitorous idea around in my head about what it might feel like to – omigod, what am I like! – *kiss* Marcus . . . and immediately felt shivery with guilt at the very idea.

And then, as if I didn't feel bad *enough*, I spot Mrs Beige Cardie parked up in-between the burger van and the wicker-work craft stall, and her whole, worrying prediction for a rubbish summer comes flooding back and slaps me as hard in the face as the mud-ball did in the middle of my back.

Now here I am, sitting hunched next to Cameron, thinking how uncomplicated things would be if I was going out with someone as relaxed and friendly as him. . .

I am a very, *very* bad person indeed.

"I think. . . I think it's over," I hear myself speak out loud.

"What's over?" asks Cameron in his kind voice, gently smoothing my hair away from my face like I'm a little girl.

"It might be all over between me and Dean!"

There, I've said it. The weird and terrifying thought that I've been trying my best not to think, never mind *say* out loud. I glance at Cameron to see what he makes of that (he's heard me witter on about Dean often enough over the last few weeks), but it's hard to tell; a dart of sun has peeked through the dull, grey clouds and is reflecting off his glasses, so all I can see is two red-nosed versions of me in distorted miniature.

"Are you sure, Mol?" he quizzes me. "'Cause everyone can have a row from time to time. It doesn't mean it's all over!"

He's so sweet and kind, he really is. How could Jude have possibly called him a creep? I love her dearly but my best mate clearly has no taste (not to mention common sense) when it comes to lads.

"I'm sure," I nod tremulously. "It wasn't just a fight. It's lots of things."

Including a girl called Stevie, who's up for "anything". . .

"Good."

"What?" I blink at Cameron, unsure what he means.

To my complete and utter shock, Cameron chooses to answer my question with body language only, lunging himself forcefully at me and suctioning his mouth to mine with all the strength of a limpet anchoring itself to a rock during a tidal wave. No matter how hard I push with my hands, his sloppy lips seem superglued to my face.

They only release (with a disgusting slurp) when an angry voice demands to know what the hell we're doing when we're supposed to be working.

I've never been so glad to see Danielle the psychotically dangerous driver in my life.

"You know, it *is* a little bit red," says Shaunna, peering at the skin around my mouth. "You're lucky he didn't leave a bruise."

"God, what if he'd given me a love-bite?" I wince, gazing at my still-startled face in the mirror Shaunna had handed me. "I mean, a love-bite on my chin and half my face: what would people have said?"

"Specially Dean!" grins Shaunna.

"Oh, don't. . ." I hide my face in my hands.

I feel so stupid for even *more* reasons than I did this morning. When I bolted round here to Shaunna's the minute the bus had dropped me back in town, she'd told me all about the call she'd had from Dean last night; the call where he poured his heart out to her, telling her he thought he'd messed everything up with me because he hadn't understood what an awkward situation I was in with my parents. He'd sworn her to secrecy, after telling her he was going to surprise me tonight with flowers and apologies and a brand new locket. . .

Unluckily for Dean, Shaunna's resolve to keep his secret lasted precisely two seconds, as soon as all my woes of the day came tumbling out. . .

"So Jude was right, then!" Shaunna suddenly grins, as she passes me a cover-up stick out of her make-up bag.

"About Cameron having a thing for me?" I shudder.

"Yeah, that – *and* the fact that he *was* a creep!" she laughs.

Yeah, a creep who not only pounced on me with no warning but got us both sacked into the bargain. Urgh. . . how could Danielle get it so wrong?

How could she mistake me trying to wriggle free for being in the throes of unadulterated passion?

Oh, the shame. . .

"But Shaunna, how can I tell my parents and Dean that I got booted out of my job because I was caught in a so-called snog! It's going to sound so *weird*!"

I can tell Shaunna sees what I mean. She leans back on her bed, bites her lip and mulls this one over.

"Listen," she replies after a few seconds' serious thinking. "You know how lying is bad?"

"Of course!" I frown. Is she mistaking me for Mia, with this back-to-basics lecture on morals?

"Well, everyone's allowed a little white lie in an emergency, aren't they?" she declares, curling her feet underneath her on her duvet.

"I suppose," I shrug.

"Let's call this an emergency, then."

"You mean, lie?"

"Exactly. Tell everyone *you* chucked the job, because you couldn't stand it. Tell them that it was doing your head in and you were scared you were going to get pneumonia or dengue fever or something after wading thigh-deep in mud day after day. Tell them you were petrified that you'd end up in the same hospital ward that *I* was in

 122

thanks to that woman Danielle's non-existent driving skills."

I nodded slowly. That *could* work . . . apart from one little loose end.

"What about my dad? He got me the job, through his friend who owns the marketing firm, remember?"

"Your dad'll never find out anything from him! Like you said, the bloke *owns* the company; you never even met him – only one of his lowly assistants!" Shaunna reasons (very reasonably). "That guy Simon who originally hired you; he'll just call up one of the others who went for the job. And wham-bam – *they*'ll be standing in a muddy field with a corny T-shirt on instead of you by this time tomorrow! *And* you'll never have to wear white jeans again!"

She's good at this, she really is. I'm starting to feel slightly better, specially now I know (via Shaunna) that my love-life isn't completely down the dumper quite yet. Yep, thanks to Shaunna (*and* her cover-up stick, *and* the loan of a spare pair of jeans and a T-shirt to change into), I'm starting to feel a tiny flutter of positivity creeping back into my soul.

"Oh, hey!" Shaunna cries out, suddenly grabbing something off her bedside table and shoving it towards me. "I've been meaning to show you this for ages! *That's* the one: that's the very caravan me and Jude will be staying in. Check out how close it is to the beach!"

I stare down at the circled photo on the turned back page of the brochure on my lap and frown.

"But I thought . . . I mean, it's just. . ." I bluster in confusion.

"Thought what?" asks Shaunna.

I can't say.

I can't tell Shaunna – who's just done a really brilliant job of bolstering up my flagging *life* – that I'm hurt because I was dumb enough to assume that she and Jude had dumped the idea of the holiday when they knew I wasn't coming.

How big-headed am I? That is, *apart* from being gullible, ratty, stupid, a terrible sister, two-faced and a complete mug.

Anyone got anything else I can beat myself up with?

124

chapter twelve

Counting my blessings (oh yeah?)

Date: *Friday 16th August*

Frame of mind: *Positive(ly awful)*

Twists of Fate: *Lists and lists...*

GOOD STUFF...
1. *I have a lovely boyfriend.*
2. *I have good friends who like me for who I am.*
3. *I have quite a nice nose.*

My project for the morning: writing lists.

It's not too exciting, but I might as well get on with it, as there's not much else to do apart from clear up the breakfast clutter like I promised, now that Mum and Dad have gone to work and Mia's off to some summer club at her school.

The list project is Jude and Shaunna's idea – they say that I've gone from being this calm, sensible person to blissed-out babe (i.e. Mental Molly), and now I'm just a moping misery-guts. They reckon that by doing this list thing, it might help me *think* myself a little happier again. (Shaunna apparently read about it in some feel-good magazine feature when she was at the dentist's this week.)

So, the plan is, while my friends are slaving away over a hot dishwasher or stacking a shelf or three at work today, I have the task of writing down all the good stuff and bad stuff in my life, and the three of us are going to sit and go over it tonight, in-between eating pizza and watching the latest Nicole Kidman movie on video.

The trouble is, I think the point of the whole exercise is that I'm supposed to go *wow!* with inspiration when I notice that the "Good Stuff" list far outweighs the "Bad Stuff" list. But at the moment I seem to have *three* things in the "Good Stuff" column and – let me count – twenty-*eight* under "Bad Stuff".

Maybe I should read through some of the "Bad

Stuff" list again and see if I can cross anything out before Jude and Shaunna read it and tell me off for not trying hard enough.

Let's see, here's a few at random:

1. Not able to hold down a summer job.

2. Haven't told Dean and M&D the truth about losing summer job.

5. Have freaky-coloured hair.

7. Have let some fake psychic put a downer on my summer.

11. Still get my lefts and rights muddled up.

12. Still keeping stum about Dublin hotel being booked, in hope that M&D change their minds.

18. Am jealous of Shaunna and Jude going on holiday without me.

20. Started biting nails again after having stopped for a whole year. . .

See? All of those are a fact, whether I like it or not. So they can't come off the list. There must be something else I could dump.

14. Dean's ring is making my finger go green.

OK, maybe that one seems a bit trivial. But it's true – the tiny heart-shaped pinkie-ring Dean gave me two weeks ago when we made up (he thought it was more romantic than the locket, he said) is not only making my finger go a strange shade, but it's itching like crazy too. Last night, just before I went to bed, I had to wriggle it off my pinkie, it got so bad, and I did wonder – for a split-second – if that wasn't some terrible omen for me and Dean, specially in the light of. . .

28. Can't get over this weird feeling about that girl Stevie.

And who can blame me? Yeah, things have *almost* got back to normal for me and Dean the last fortnight or so, but then I saw the text message that came through on his mobile when he was watching *Star Trek* with Mia yesterday evening. . . *Hi D-No! Coming out to play? Call me – Stevie.*

I didn't confront "D-No" about it. I just took great pleasure in deleting both Stevie's message and her number from the phone list on his mobile while Dean and Mia were watching the forces of evil being repulsed by Spock and Co in my front room.

Great. . . I think, splatting my head down on to the kitchen table and feeling the toast crumbs indent into my forehead.

I'm going to have to add that to my "Bad Stuff" list now;

29. Have started deleting my boyfriend's text messages because I'm a jealous idiot, and I don't know if I've actually got anything to be jealous about.

Or is that in fact two *separate* points? One, that I hide messages, and two, that I'm jealous. . .

Good grief: I'll have a list that's the length of a roll of wallpaper by the time Jude and Shaunna come round. All of it moany and miserable, like the moany misery-guts I am.

"So what are you up to this weekend?" a voice suddenly makes me jump – then I realize I've just leant my arm on the volume control on the remote for the portable telly and tuned into a cheery end-of-the-programme bit of banter between two impossibly bouncy breakfast TV presenters.

"Well, it's going to be a busy one for me!" the orange-faced woman replies to her orange-faced co-presenter. "I've got simply lists and lists of things to do!"

Lists and lists, I think numbly, gazing down at the two sheets of scrawled-on paper in front of me.

"Me too!" the male presenter booms merrily. "Don't know about you, viewers, but if you're lucky enough to have lots of time on your hands this weekend, I'd say, count your blessings and get out in that sunshine – you never know how long it's going to last, do you!"

"Ha, ha! No, you certainly don't! Ha, ha!" chuckles the female presenter, as if Mr Orange has just cracked the most hilarious joke in the cosmiverse.

But as they call out their fond farewells over the bingly-bongly theme tune, I suddenly feel something go *clunk* in my brain.

It's like the fickle finger of Fate has pressed "replay" in my head.

"*. . .lists and lists . . . if you're lucky enough to have lots of time on your hands this weekend . . . count your blessings . . . get out in that sunshine. . .!*"

"I don't need to sit festering in the house, poring over endless lists to sort myself out!" I mutter, standing up from the table and brushing the toast crumbs from my forehead. "I need to get out!"

In two seconds flat, I've pulled on my trainers, grabbed my bag, headed out the front door and startled the postman with a ridiculously cheery hello.

(Hey, maybe my future lies in presenting day-time TV shows. . .?)

"Molly? It's me. Where are you? It sounds really noisy. . ."

"It's just a bus passing," I raise my voice so that Shaunna can hear me on her mobile. "I'm on my way home – nearly at my house."

I'd practically jumped out of my skin when she rang a second ago; inspired by a day's worth of

 130

hanging out in the park, I was doing that old kid thing of trying to walk along the pavement without stepping on any cracks.

"Oh," Shaunna grunts in reply. "Listen, Mol – sorry, but you're going to have to do tonight without me."

"Why?" I ask, my shoulders sinking in disappointment.

I was really looking forward to seeing her and Jude. I couldn't wait to tell them how the list project had worked, in a round-about way. A long walk, a big, old think – that had done me the world of good. I'd found myself in the park, sat myself on a bench, and spent literally hours watching kids play, dogs bound and grass grow, all the while trying to unravel some of the tangles in my head. And once I'd had enough of the park bench, I lay down on the grass and studied the clouds drifting across the sky. I'd marvelled at the great big universe and managed to put my own petty, piddly problems into perspective.

And then I'd pulled out my Filofax and pen, and started scribbling my alternative list: the "Count Your Blessings" list. It's full of great stuff, like. . .

1. I may have freaky-coloured hair, but at least I have hair and not alopecia.

2. So I lost my summer job – so what? Hated it anyway.

3. Dean's ring might make my finger go green, but at least it proves he loves me (and not this Stevie person).

I'd got a real kick out of putting it all together, and now Shaunna wasn't going to be around to give me a gold star for effort. She'd better have a pretty good reason for blowing me out. . .

"It's so corny – Mum and Dad are insisting they take me out for a meal tonight to celebrate," she explains, but I'm no further enlightened.

"Celebrate what?" I ask, as I approach our familiar black metal front gate.

"My exam marks, stupid!" Shaunna laughs. "Didn't you get my text? I did 'excellently' – at least that's what Dad says! What about you? How did it go? What about that maths exam?"

The postman . . . the bundle of envelopes in his hand when I was on my way out earlier . . . I'd totally forgotten that the results were due out today.

"Damn!" I cry out, realizing I've just stood on my first crack in the pavement after avoiding them all the way home from the park.

"What? You didn't get good marks?" I hear Shaunna ask in concern.

 132

"No – it's not that," I shake my head, as if she can see me. "I haven't checked the post today. Hold on, Shaun—"

My key's in the door, I'm stepping inside, I can see the ominous brown envelope on the hall table from here. My heart is thundering in my chest. I'm remembering that fraught last day of term (and exams) which also happened to be the first day I'd ever experienced the feeling that someone, somewhere, was trying to let me know that everything (including my maths exam) was going to be all right.

"I'm opening it now. It says. . ."

"What? What did you get?" I hear Shaunna quizzing me.

But I don't get the chance to tell her that my exam marks range from a handful of stunning just-scraped-throughs, to a truly *awesome* fail (maths). That's because I'm suddenly distracted by the rustle of paper, and turn to see that my mother is already home and is currently standing in the kitchen doorway, holding up a piece of paper headed "Bad Stuff".

"You know, Molly, I'm particularly interested in hearing more about point number two and point number twelve," she says to me dryly.

"Mol? What's up?"

"I'll have to call you back, Shaunna," I whisper quickly.

Help.

If I'm not grounded for life after this, then I'll *really* be counting my blessings. . .

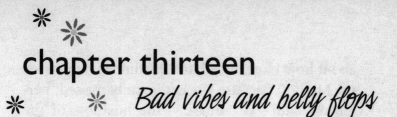

chapter thirteen

Bad vibes and belly flops

Date: Monday 19th August

Frame of mind: Paranoid

Twists of Fate: A cruel one

There was a change to the advertised programme on Friday night: pizza, video and gossiping with Jude was hastily replaced with humble pie, grovelling and a stern talking-to from Mum and Dad.

The upshot was: bad exam results they can just about live with (as long as I cross-my-heart-and-hope-to-die promise to try harder at my resit); lying they can't. So now they know everything about how I lost my job ("Why didn't you just tell us, Molly?" Because I was too embarrassed, perhaps?) and – of course – the business of the non-cancelled holiday. Before I slinked off to my room, I'd promised them I'd a) cancel the holiday immediately, b) cool things off for a while with Dean, and c) never lie to them again.

Oops.

"Where's Adam?" asks Dean, crouching down beside me and the others on the grass, while keeping his eyes firmly on the splashing, squealing hordes dive-bombing into the shimmering swimming pool.

Erm, as you might have guessed, I'm not in actual fact at Jude's house, where my parents assume I am spending the day commiserating over our dodgy exam results. (Just as well neither me or Jude planned to be brain surgeons or rocket scientists.)

Yep, this *is* the lido, and that *is* Dean talking – Dean, who I'm supposed to be taking a break from.

"He's over in the toddler pool with Bethany," Shaunna replies, squirting more suncream on to her shoulders.

"Oh, yeah? Well, that should suit Adam, since he's got the mental age of a three year old!" Dean grins. "Have you checked he's got his water wings on?"

"Hey, you! Remember that *is* Shaunna's boyfriend you're talking about!"

I shouldn't exactly need to remind Dean of that not-inconsequential fact.

"Yeah, but he's my cousin so I'm allowed to say what I like about him!" Dean shrugs and laughs. "He'd do the same for me!"

"And are you allowed to be talking to us when you should be doing your *Baywatch* thing and saving lives?"

Valid point from Jude there.

"You're right, Ju – I'd better get back to it before the supervisor spots me," says Dean, pushing himself back up into a standing position. "I just came over to say that I can't take my lunchbreak till two, Molly – I've got to go and do some cover in the indoor pool now."

"That's OK," I shrug.

To be totally honest, it's not just Dean I came to see today anyway. I'm on a spying mission, with Shaunna, Jude, Adam and his hyperactive niece as cover. Exams? I'll fret about them another day, right now I'm fretting about a girl I'm beginning to be obsessed by (much like my boyfriend, by the sound of it, and from the amount of after-work time they're still spending together).

"I just wish you'd told me you were planning

on coming today, Mol," Dean adds, blocking the sun from my face as he towers over me. "I could have swapped breaks with one of the others."

Oh, yeah? Like your new best mate Stevie, perhaps?

Thanks to working all weekend and partying (yet again) with Stevie and Co on Saturday night, Dean doesn't even seem to have noticed that we've spent precisely no time together over the last couple of days. Which is why I still haven't been able to tell him face-to-face about our little problem with my parents.

"Catch up with you later, yeah?" says Dean, striding off towards the tiled walkway round the edge of the pool.

"Those are criminally short shorts your boyfriend is wearing," Shaunna suddenly announces, lifting her sunglasses up off her nose for a better gawp as Dean walks away.

"Shaunna!" Jude gasps, indignant on my behalf.

"Well, they are! You don't mind me saying that, do you, Mol?"

Of course I don't. Shaunna is my friend and I can trust her totally. Especially since I know she doesn't fancy Dean in the least – or she wouldn't have dumped him like she did last year.

Stevie, however, is an unknown quantity. I have

 138

no idea what's going on with her and Dean. But just as there's every chance that it's nothing, there's just as much chance that she's desperate to get her over-friendly hands on my boyfriend, which makes it *not* a great time to be on a break with him. But try explaining that to my parents. . .

"Where do you think she is?" I ask.

"Who?" Jude asks distractedly, as she turns over on her tummy and struggles to unclip her bikini top without exposing any boobage.

"That Stevie person; the girl we're supposed to be spying on," Shaunna reminds her, as she tilts her face towards the sun.

"You haven't told Adam that's the real reason we're here, have you, Shaun?"

I feel I have to check that with Shaunna, thanks to a sinking feeling of dread tugging at my insides. God, how awful would *that* be? What if Adam told Dean?

"Chill out!" is all Shaunna replies, kind of annoyingly.

What's that supposed to mean? *Has* Shaunna told him or hasn't she? No . . . no, don't be stupid – she wouldn't. Still, she's making me feel like I'm overreacting, and I'm not. So, I'm going to bite my lip and shut up, just so she can see that I'm totally calm and rational about this whole Stevie thing. Whatever it is. And whoever she is.

"But where is she?" I find myself blurting out half-a-second later.

There are two lifeguards currently propped up on those metal highchairs at either end of the pool at the moment, and both are most definitely male.

"Maybe she's on duty in the indoor pool," Shaunna suggests.

"Or maybe she's not working today."

"Don't say that!" I whimper at Jude. "That'd just make today a waste of time!"

"What – hanging out with us, having a nice day out is a waste of time?" Shaunna stares accusingly over her shades at me. "Having the chance to talk over the latest parent crisis with your boyfriend is a waste of time?"

"No! You know what I mean!" I protest. "I need to check out this girl, because . . . because. . ."

"Because you're paranoid," Shaunna announces, raising her eyebrows at me.

"Shaunna!"

"Well, come on, Mol! It's true!"

I'm sure she's almost smirking, like my private life falling apart is one big joke.

Actually, I'm so stunned at Shaunna's lack of support that I glance around at Jude – who is staring

 140

down at the ground instead of looking shocked for my sake. Great, so *she* thinks I'm paranoid too.

"Why did you bother coming with me today, then?" I ask, jolting myself up into a more upright position. "Don't you *care* that Dean could be fooling around behind my back?"

"See? *That*'s why you're so paranoid," Shaunna points out in an infuriatingly matter-of-fact way. "Why are you so determined to think the worst of Dean? There's no *way* he's fooling around – he's crazy about you!"

See why I can't talk to her about Dean? What did I say about her and Jude being his number-one fans?

"What about this girl, then? How come she's so friendly with him?"

"Well, maybe that's all she is – friendly!" shrugs Shaunna. "And even if she *does* fancy him, so what? People are allowed to fancy people!"

Shaunna can be *so* maddening. Whose side is she on?

"So you think it's OK for her to come on to my boyfriend?!" I suggest.

"No, I'm just saying that . . . here – here's an example. See that guy over there?"

Still smarting, I find myself staring in the direction she's pointing in.

"The guy with the cool little dreads?" asks Jude.

"Yeah – isn't he gorgeous?" Shaunna states loudly and shamelessly. "Check the body on him!"

"Shaunna! Shh!" I suddenly whisper. "Adam's coming back over!"

I may be irritated with my friend, but I'm loyal enough to want to stop her saying something she'll regret.

"So what?" she replies. "Hey, Adam – I was just saying, that guy over there, he's pretty gorgeous, isn't he?"

Adam flops, dripping, down on to a spread-out towel and squints over at the boy with the body.

"Yep, I guess. And nice pecs. Not as good as mine, of course," he answers casually, lifting his puny arm and flexing a non-existent muscle that Bethany tries to squeeze.

Adam crumples under her touch, feigning pain, while Bethany – and Shaunna and Jude – get the giggles. Doesn't he get it? Doesn't he see that his girlfriend is drooling over another guy?

"All I'm trying to say," Shaunna turns her smile away from Adam's antics and back to me, "is that it's OK for people to fancy other people, as long as they don't do anything about it."

"Unlike that creep Cameron," Jude butts in.

"Well, he's a *prime* example of someone going too far," Shaunna nods. "But it's like you fancying

142

that guy in the hospital, Molly. There's no harm in you having a bit of a two-second crush on him, because you had no intention of following it up, did you?"

I'm mortified – how can she come out with private, girl-sharing stuff like this in front of Adam? And what's more, I don't really get what she's trying to say; all I know is that I feel like I'm being lectured to, and I've had enough of that from my parents lately.

"What are you on about, Shaunna?" I ask bluntly, ducking to look at her better, now Bethany has picked up her sheep-shaped backpack and is hugging it to her soggy swimsuit right between us.

"All I'm saying is, I think you're getting too wound up about this. Even if this girl fancies Dean – and you don't know if she does – you can't blame her. Dean is very cute—"

"Not as cute as me, of course," Adam can't help wisecrack.

I feel like grabbing Bethany's woolly backpack and shoving it in his gob to shut him up. And another thing – I wish Bethany would stop staring at me, it's very unnerving.

"—but it doesn't mean *he* would look at *her* twice in that way," Shaunna concludes.

"It's all 'buts' and 'maybes'! You don't *know* what could be going on!" I hiss at Shaunna, darting my head from side to side to see her past Bethany's still earnestly staring face.

"Exactly! And until you know something, I think you should stop flipping out!" says Shaunna.

Aaargh! I want to blast something smart and cutting and clever right back at her, but my brain is too scrambled with rage to get the right words together in a coherent sentence.

"Snap!"

Huh? Bethany is now practically nose-to-nose with me and has placed her white woolly, sheep-shaped bag up against my ear. What am I supposed to do? *Listen* to it?

"Snap!" she repeats, now pointing at the bag and then at my head.

"Aw!" I hear Jude coo. "She thinks your hair's the same colour as. . ."

I don't hang around to listen to the end of that – who needs to be told they look like a sheep? What I *do* need is to get away from the bad vibes of my so-called friends and cool off. And the quickest way to do that is to take a dive off the deep end of the swimming pool.

"Come on, Molly! Don't be like that!" I hear

Shaunna call out behind me, as I stomp off towards the beckoning blue ripples.

In a millisecond, I'll be under water, away from her lecturing voice. Thank goodness. . .

"Omigod, is she OK?" I hear Dean's panic-tinged voice.

"She's fine – she's just getting her breath back," says a soothing female voice. "You're all right, aren't you, Molly?"

I nod a tiny nod, fixing my eyes on the light dangling from the ceiling above. That's as much as I can manage, as I'm presently finding it hard enough to concentrate on clearing the fog in my head and getting my heartbeat slowed down from the high-octane tap-dance it's currently doing.

"What happened?" Dean's voice floats somewhere above me.

What happened? I'm not sure myself – one minute I'm arcing into a graceful dive, the next minute . . . there's a pain in my stomach and I'm choking.

"Don't know really. I was just coming out to let Craig off for a break, and I saw her do this really bad belly flop into the water," says the voice that isn't Dean's. "It looked pretty painful, so I watched for a second, and when she didn't come up, I knew she was in trouble, so I got straight in there."

Me? I belly flopped? Then nearly *drowned*? In front of *everyone*? Oh the shame. . .

"Thank God you rescued her, Stevie, that's all I can say," Dean's wobbly voice sighs.

Stevie? I belly flopped, nearly drowned, and was rescued by *Stevie*?

Looks like everyone – including Fate – is having a bloody good laugh at my expense. . .

chapter fourteen

The hot new hairdo...

Date: *Saturday 25th August*

Frame of mind: *Adventurous*

Twists of Fate: *Disastrous*

"Uh . . . got any holidays planned?" I hear myself being asked, as the beltingly hot heat lamp is finally lifted off my head after what feels like *days. . .*

"Got any holidays planned?": it's the bog-standard hairdresser question, isn't it? The one they ask *every* customer. (Only usually it comes without the "Uh. . ." bit at the beginning.)

If you think about it, a hairdresser might have an average of six customers a day, which makes thirty customers a week; and if you multiply *that* by twelve months (give or take a few weeks off for – ha! – holidays), it means a hairdresser asks the "Got any holidays planned?" question roughly 1,500 times over the course of a year.

That's when you're talking about your *normal* hairdresser.

Kerry, the girl who's (supposedly) putting warm, golden lowlights in my hair has probably asked this question only once (i.e. to me, just now), since she looks about the same age as me, has told me she only started the job on Monday, and sounds very, *very* nervous.

Mind you, I'm pretty nervous about answering her question. If you asked my parents on my behalf, they would say, no – Molly has no holiday plans. If you asked Dean . . . well, he booked the ferry tickets to Ireland yesterday and has cleared it with his dad to have the car next weekend.

Oh, God – what a mess. . .

But before the whole world turns all Shaunna on me and tells me off, I *can* explain why Dean is under the impression that we're still going to Dublin together. Here's an edited version of the conversation I had with him, right after Stevie left

148

us sitting together in the First Aid room at the lido on Monday. . .

Dean: "I'll phone your mum and let her know what's happened."

Me: "No! Don't do that!" (Translation: "But she'll find out I saw you behind her back!")

Dean: "Well, then, I'll see the supervisor and see if I can get off now so I can take you home."

Me: "No! I mean – it's OK. Adam and the girls will do that." (Translation: "Being spotted at my house would *definitely* qualify as seeing you behind my parents' backs!")

Dean (reluctantly): "Well, all right, but I'll come round and see you straight after work."

Me: "No!" (Translation: "NO!!!")

And then it all came tumbling out; all the stuff about Mum and Dad thinking I was lying to them; about how they'd more-or-less banned me from seeing Dean for a couple of weeks as a punishment.

And then – bless him – Dean's whole face crumpled. He's always the good guy; always the boy who's respectful and friendly to my parents; who's part of the furniture round our house, getting his tea there and fighting over the remote control with Mia (Mia likes her sci-fi stuff LOUD). He was genuinely hurt.

Add to that the fact that Dean had looked *frantic* with worry since the moment I'd managed to spit half the swimming pool out of my lungs and focus on him, and I found myself coming over all protective. Next thing, I'm hugging him as much as he's hugging me, all the while desperately assuring him that everything would be all right. I heard my voice blurting out that we'd still be able to go to Ireland, that Mum and Dad were mad at me for not being straight with them – that was all – but now that it was all out in the open, all I had to do was play the dutiful daughter for a couple of weeks, take my punishment, and then they'd be fine about me going away with him.

Yeah, *right*.

I don't know why Dean chose to believe that (he's *way* too trusting, let me tell you), but he did, and he gave me the biggest, most gorgeous, bearhug of a cuddle. How could I resist? It was obvious that it was me he loved, not Stevie. (Who, incidentally, was a plain-ish, mousy-haired tomboy, I was quite pleased to note, through my chlorine-drenched haze.)

It'll all work out somehow, I'm sure. I'll try and talk to Mum over the weekend, if I can get her on her own and avoid the strength-in-numbers pairing of her and Dad together. I'll appeal to her better judgement. I'll plead true love. I'll promise to do everyone's laundry for a year, if that's what it takes.

"Actually, I'm going to Dublin next Saturday," I tell the hairdresser, hoping that if I sound confident enough, then it'll seem more of a reality.

"Dublin . . . where's that again?" she asks, as she leads me over to a sink.

Uh-oh.

I hope she's better at doing hair than she is at geography. . .

Wrong.

"Oh, Molly!" my mother sighs breathily, frowning at me for the thousandth time. "Why did you do it?"

"I *told* you," I reply tearfully. "I *hate* having white hair! I *just* wanted a change!"

Adam's niece Bethany may only be three, but she's got a lot to answer for. After all, the mess I was in was all down to her comparing my hair to a sheep's fleece the other day. (White? Dull? No thanks. . .)

But then again, I guess it was my own fault for being swayed by the ad in the hairdresser's window offering free cuts and colours if you let juniors run riot on your head. And being a penniless mug who's saving up for a holiday I'm not supposed to be going on, I was easily won over.

"Can you warm it up a bit?" That was the phrase I'd used to explain what I wanted Kerry to do to my ice-maiden locks. What a joke – instead of rich, golden lowlights, I now have white hair with vivid pinky-orange stripes, as well as very possibly third-degree burns to my scalp.

"Don't scratch!" Mum warns me, as the skin on my head and around the edge of my face burns hotter than a furnace, and itches worse than a carpet-bombing of mosquito bites. "It should be your turn to see the doctor soon!"

I'm back in Casualty, sitting two seats up from where me and Mia whiled away a couple of hours not so long ago after her goat bite. I should have a season ticket for this place. It's a wonder the hospital didn't put up bunting and a "Welcome back, Molly!" sign above the front entrance. . .

Speaking about that, they say things happen in threes, don't they? So first there was Shaunna and her amazing trapeze tumbling act (my fault); then there was the Mia/goat incident (my fault); and now here I am, sitting in the waiting room, burning up with strange chemicals and humiliation, and it's nobody's fault but mine. Maybe it's time to ditch three as my lucky number. . .

"I look terrible, don't I?" I find myself suddenly sniffling.

"It won't be so bad once you've got some medication," Mum says in her soothing mumsy voice. "And with a bit of make-up . . . and maybe a hat. . ."

That's it.

I'm the Elephant Man, only with orange stripes and vivid red blotches. What did I do to deserve this? (Er, lie to everyone I love. . .?)

"Listen, Molly, I was thinking," says Mum, slipping a cool hand into one of mine. "I know me and your dad came down a bit heavy on you recently – grounding you and everything – but. . ."

But? I say to myself, hardly daring to breath.

". . .but what I thought was, if you want to go to the seaside with Jude and Shaunna next weekend, then that would be all right with me and. . ."

She tails off, mainly because I've started blubbing, and I don't really know why. She's so lovely, my mum, she really is. And there's nothing I'd like better than to go away with my best friends in the world. (You should have seen how they fussed and fretted over me on Monday when they took me home!) Itching and burning pain aside, I'm suddenly happier than I've been in weeks. It's like a weight's been lifted off my shoulders, it's like everything is OK . . . apart from the fact that I've got this secret pact to go on holiday with Dean.

Oh, God. . .

"Hey, Molly, what's up? I thought you'd be pleased!" Mum gasps at the sight of my face (not a pretty picture *before* I scrunched it up).

"I. . . I. . . I. . ." I hiccup, getting nowhere near a sentence that makes sense.

"Tissue?" says a rich, deep voice, as a thick wad of green, industrial-strength paper towel is wafted under my dribbling nose.

"Thanks," I mumble weepily, grabbing a bundle as my emotions crash into each other and my eyes well up with tears.

"That's very sweet of you," I hear Mum say to whoever. "I think she's suffering from a bit of shock."

"No problem. That's the way it is in here. So how's the little sister doing? Survived the goat attack, has she?"

He's crouching down in front of me, this boy in blue. If I could just stop crying for five seconds, I know that black blur on Marcus's brown arm would reveal itself as a tiny heart. Almost a perfect match for the small, green, heart-shaped stain my ring left on my pinkie.

As Bethany would say, "Snap!"

"Er, Molly, isn't that your mobile?" Mum's voice interrupts me dopily grinning at Marcus.

"Text. . ." I mumble, vaguely aware of the twinkly noise my phone is making, compared to its usual jolly *Bagpuss* ringing tone.

"Might be important!" Marcus smiles, as he pulls a marker pen out of his top pocket and starts doodling something on one of the green paper towels.

"OK," I smile at him, doing as he says and digging my mobile out of my back pocket.

(I wince as I realize that smiling actually hurts my mildly burnt face.)

Hi, Mol! I read. *Bit confused since we last met. Want 2 meet up? Mmm . . . miss U. Luv. . . C xxx.*

In my pain-induced blur, I struggle to understand this.

"C": who is "C"? Who is this "C" who loves and misses me? I don't know anyone whose name begins with "C", apart from Clare that I used to work with on the Milk Mobile . . . and . . . oh, God.

"Everything all right?" Mum asks me gently.

"Yes," I mumble, pressing "delete" on my mobile and watching Cameron the creep's message vanish into nothingness. . .

155

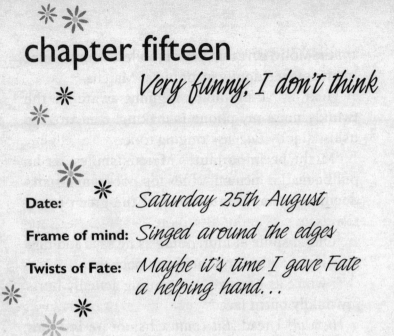

chapter fifteen

Very funny, I don't think

Date: *Saturday 25th August*

Frame of mind: *Singed around the edges*

Twists of Fate: *Maybe it's time I gave Fate a helping hand...*

You know what would be nice right now?

Not winning the lottery (although that would be sweet); not waking up tomorrow and finding that my hair has miraculously turned naturally brown/black/red/golden (anything apart from white blonde with luminous stripes).

I'm not greedy, or unrealistic. The only thing I think would be genuinely, truly nice right now is this: if all I had to worry about was some dumb maths exam.

Looking back to the beginning of summer, it now seems totally ridiculous that I ever worried about that at all. The sleepless nights; the fledgling ulcer; the panic-blindness every time I opened a textbook. . . I mean, I've never scored good marks in maths in my life, so the chance of me passing the exam was about as remote as my face turning up on the cover of *Marie Claire* any time soon. So why did I stress out about failing when it was a foregone conclusion?

But compared to now, my time in exam hell was a breeze. My entire summer has been one long complication, and right now, the pressing problems currently vying to give me premature grey hair (I *wish*) are as follows:

1) I look like one of those poor lab bunnies from the PETA leaflets – you know; the ones that have raw red patches of skin showing through their white fur after heartless testers have dribbled toxic chemicals all over them. (My heartless tester happened to be called Kerry.)

2) My mother is really annoyed with me for insisting I have to see Jude this evening. She thinks I should be resting after my hair trauma.

What she doesn't know is that I'm lying again: I'm not with Jude, I'm with Dean, again.

3) I'm with Dean, again, because I need to untangle some of the knots I've got myself into, and that means coming clean to him about our holiday (or lack of it) next week. Only it's kind of hard to talk to him, considering we're now sitting in the beer garden of the pub next door to the lido, with a whole posse of noisy lifeguards.

4) So Stevie looked plain, mousy-haired and tomboy-ish last time I saw her (when I was being dragged from the pool)? Not out of uniform, she doesn't. I'm staring at her now, marvelling at the fact that I didn't even recognize my saviour when I first walked in here. With her shiny hair unleashed from its ponytail, a large helping of make-up, and a tiny pink vest-top that her boobs are straining to escape from, she looks the exact opposite of a tomboy – a fact which all the lads around the table seem to appreciate. Does that include Dean?

5) I'm being stalked (by text at least) by creepy Cameron.

See what I mean about the maths exam?

"Love the bandanna!" Stevie leans across the wooden picnic table to tell me.

"Thanks," I try and smile, but that's still a bit of a tricky manoeuvre for my scorched skin. Which is at this minute itching and nipping in equal measure under the scarf I've tied round my head and the make-up I've slapped on my face.

I wish this low evening sun would hurry up and sink – daylight can't be doing anything flattering to me and my freaky epidermis.

"Hey, Stevie," says a boy called Jez, who's sitting on the other side of Dean. "I wouldn't lean forward like that if I were you . . . not in *that* top!"

"Oooh, help!" shrieks Stevie, slapping her arms across her chest and straightening up. "I'm always doing that! Think I'd be safer in a big Aran jumper!"

Yeah, but you wouldn't get so much attention from the boys, then, would you? I think darkly, while I smile but stare dead-eyed at Stevie through my shades.

Yes, I know it's pretty mean to think badly of someone who may well have saved my life (perhaps . . . I might still have managed to bumble to the surface without any help), but I can't help thinking that Stevie was more interested in revealing a chasm of cleavage to Dean there than she was in giving me a compliment. And I know you shouldn't judge people on looks (and body language, and excessive cleavage) alone, but Stevie sure seems like the kind of girl who wouldn't faff around with yes, no, maybes, unlike me. . .

"All right?" Dean smiles at me, while everyone else is still busy guffawing at Stevie's "hilarious" comment.

I notice his eyes are darting over my bandanna and my face, and I know he's wondering why I'm wearing more make-up than usual. I want to tell him all about what happened to me today at the hairdresser (and the rest), but now is definitely not the time.

"Uh-huh," I mutter back. "It's just that I wanted it to be just the two of us. . ."

That's what I'd expected it to be. I'd made a whispered call to Dean's mobile earlier, once I got home from hospital with Mum, and asked if we could meet. Dean said fine, and suggested this place. Only he didn't tell me he'd be bringing half the lido along with him.

"I thought it would be good for you to meet everyone properly," he says under his breath, as Stevie continues her one-woman comedy routine. For some reason she has now stuck a beermat on her forehead and is laughing like a drain.

Translation: Dean wants me to meet everyone properly, i.e. when I'm not embarrassing him by being some belly-flopping saddo who nearly drowns in front of all his buddies.

"Yeah, but I really need to talk to you, Dean. . ."

160

"After I finish this drink, OK?" he smiles, slipping his hand over mine. "By the way, why haven't you been wearing the ring I bought you?"

"Keep forgetting," I mumble, finding a white lie tripping off my tongue yet again. . . .

I like disabled toilets. They're really roomy (none of that bashing-your-knees stuff you get in normal cubicles as you try to squeeze your way in and close the impossibly tight-fitting doors).

And, as well as keeping your knees safe from harm, the other advantage of disabled toilets is that they generally come with their own basin and mirror, so you can do your make-up without anyone else putting you off by gawping at you as they queue to use the loos.

Not that I'm putting on make-up just now – I can't bear to catch sight of myself in any reflective surfaces, and anyway, if I wore any more make-up my head would drop forward with the weight of it. What I *am* doing is taking my time, using the disabled toilet as a refuge from Dean's loud and lairy new friends, and trying to scrub the reluctant green heart-shaped stain off my pinkie.

God, I feel so nervous . . . isn't it mad to feel nervous about talking to your own boyfriend, who you've been going out with for nearly a whole

161

year? Who you've shared all your stories and secrets with? Who you were just about to go on holiday – all alone – with? But my heart's palpitating like crazy at the idea of blowing out Dublin. Not to mention telling Dean about the so-called snog that got me fired from my summer job. After all, if I don't tell him that then I can't tell him about creepy Cameron's creepy message – and I need him to know about it in case he wants to come over all protective and tell Cameron to leave me alone. That's *if* I can't get that through to Cameron myself. (For the last couple of hours I've been fretting myself silly trying to come up with a suitable reply to his text message. I thought about "Bog off" but I'd like to seem smarter than that.)

". . .she's a bit, well, weird? Isn't she?"

I suddenly tune into a girl's voice, somewhere beyond the chipboard cubicle door I'm hovering behind.

How funny! I think, holding my breath and trying to listen in, above the sound of the hand-dryer whirring into life out by the main sinks. *Wonder who she's bitching about?*

"Weird? She's weird with knobs on!" cackles a vaguely familiar voice in response. "What's with her face? It looks . . . bizarre!"

"And that bandanna! It wouldn't be so bad if she hadn't tucked *all* her hair under it. When you told her it looked nice, I nearly burst out laughing!"

"Tell me about it! You know something? I don't know what the hell Dean sees in her!"

Oh. It's *me* they're bitching about.

"Me neither! I just don't get it! I mean, he's *so* cute and funny. And OK, so she's *sort* of pretty and everything, but she's just a bit. . ."

"Weird?" cackles Stevie.

"Yeah!" laughs the other voice. "Aw, poor you, Stevie. Couldn't you pick someone who *doesn't* have a weird girlfriend to have a crush on?"

"Hey, you can't help who you fall for!" I hear Stevie sigh. "And anyway, who says he'll have a weird girlfriend for much longer? Not if *I* have anything to do with it!"

I don't start breathing again until I hear the cackle of laughter disappear outside into the pub corridor and beyond.

The mirror above the sink feels cool when I thump my burning hot forehead up against it. . .

"Shaunna – I'm coming on holiday with you next week," I pant down the phone, as I run as far from the pub as I can, as fast as I can.

"What?" I hear Shaunna squeal in surprise.

"That's OK, isn't it?" I ask, suddenly realizing that maybe I'm pushing my luck, barging in on a holiday I'd nearly managed to spoil in the first place.

"Jeez, Mol – of *course* you can come! Me and Jude would *love* you to! It wasn't going to be the same without you!"

I feel choked, honest I do.

"I'll sleep on the floor!" I tell her. "I don't mind! Just as long as I can be with you and Jude!"

"You don't have to sleep on the floor, you idiot!" Shaunna laughs. "It's a caravan! And you know what caravans are like – everything folds out and converts into a bed, even the kitchen cupboards!"

See, *this* is what I need; Shaunna and her silliness – no complications or hassles or girls fancying your boyfriend.

"Brilliant!" I gasp, spotting a bus that goes near my house and waving it down.

"But what's happened with Dean and Dublin? Is that definitely a no-go? Are your parents not budging? What's poor Dean saying about it?"

"Poor" Dean is saying nothing. Probably because he's got his face wrapped around Stevie's right now. Hey, maybe *she'd* fancy taking a trip to Dublin in my place. . .

"Um, my bus is here, Shaun. I'll fill you in later, yeah?"

"Are you all right Molly? You sound weird. . ."

Oh, not *that* word again.

"Bad day on the planet. I'll explain later – I'll phone you when I get home," I pant, as I pay the driver and hear the reception starting to crackle.

"Quick – give me edited highlights to keep me going till then!" Shaunna demands.

"OK. . ." I reply, bounding up the stairs to the top deck. "How about, I've been mutilated by a hairdresser; I've just seen my boyfriend flirting with Stevie—"

Oh, yes: after who-knows-how-long hiding out in the loos, I'd finally taken a deep breath and headed back out into the beer garden, only to see Stevie sitting so close to Dean that she was practically perched on his knee. From the way he was laughing he was obviously *loving* every second of her coming on to him.

Cue me turning and running out of there fast, before anyone spotted me.

"Dean? Nah! You've got to be joking!"

"I'm not, Shaunna – I saw it for myself!" I tell her. She can't take his side now, can she? Not with evidence like that?

"I can't believe it!"

"And if *that* wasn't bad enough, I'm being stalked by that guy Cameron. He sent the creepiest text message earlier!"

"Omigod. . ." Shaunna gasps.

"I know," I nod to the passing view of shops and houses.

"No, I mean . . . hold on, Molly, you don't understand," Shaunna says hurriedly. "*I* sent that message!"

"Huh?"

What is she on about?

"It was a joke – I was just trying to make you laugh! Didn't you get the message straight after that? The one where I said, 'Ha, ha, ha, gotcha!'?"

"No," I fume, feeling like a total fool.

I'd got so spooked by that first message back at the hospital, I'd just switched off my phone and chucked it to the bottom of my bag till now.

"Oh, Mol! I'm *so* sorry! I didn't mean to freak you out! I was only—"

"You're breaking up, Shaunna," I say, letting another white lie slip across my lips. "I'll call you later."

Nice. I can't trust my own boyfriend with another girl, and now one of my best friends goes and plays crappy jokes on me.

I need to speak to someone who won't make a

fool of me; someone who's on my side. Jude? No –
she was probably in on Shaunna's dumb prank.
She's probably still laughing about it now.

Is there no one out there who doesn't want to
make a fool of me?

Well, maybe there's one. . .

I dive into my bag and rifle around for the green
paper towel with the phone number scrawled on it
in black marker pen. . .

chapter sixteen
Hello ... goodbye

Date: *Sunday 26th August*

Frame of mind: *Excited. No ... nervous. OK, both*

Twists of Fate: *Disastrous*

I could be a lookalike. That could be my perfect career move, which links in nicely with my less-than-sparkly exam results.

Oh, yes . . . I can see it now. The phone at my agent's will ring off the hook with requests for me to do Saturday morning telly guest spots; openings of shopping centres; appearances at county fairs (urgh, don't remind me); even just birthday parties for bouncy four year olds.

That's right, I'm all set to be the human version of old-time telly puppet favourite Bagpuss. (I've even got my own theme tune on my mobile phone.) I mean, who else can do furry white and stripy so well?

Please, *please* don't let that be the first thing that pops into Marcus's head the second he sees me. . .

"Hey," he grins.

But it's not a grin that says: "I'm laughing at you, weird girl, with your weird hair and splatchy skin". It's a grin that says: "I'm really glad you called me".

"Hi," I smile shyly, fidgeting nervously with my bandanna and barely able to look at him, as I slide into the seat opposite.

(It's been a really long time since I've been on a date and I'm not sure I can remember what I'm meant to say or do.)

"I'm really glad you called me," says Marcus, above the racket of my chair legs screeching unromantically on the tiled floor.

See? I knew that's what that grin meant!

We're in the café in the park, and I've just arrived ten minutes late for our three o'clock date this Sunday afternoon because I spent so long faffing around trying to make myself look vaguely human (i.e. less like a sickly lab bunny). Then I wised up and realized that Marcus had seen me at my worst back at the hospital – newly striped, scalded and scalped AND with teary, red-rimmed, puffy eyes and snotty nose to (mis)match. And yet he *still* went and gave me his phone number. . .

"*He* seemed very nice!" my mum had cooed on the way home that day.

You know, she'd tried to hide it from me, but I could tell she was thrilled that I had a date with Marcus. Last night, she'd fumed with concern when I insisted on going out to see Jude/Dean (maybe she suspected the truth). Today, she was practically helping me pick out my clothes.

Actually, in a way, it was almost sad to see how much she wanted to see Dean relegated to the category of ex-boyfriend. She – and Dad (not to mention Mia) – had always seemed so fond of Dean; treated him like another member of the family (presents at Christmas, an ever-open sign on the fridge door, the end of the sofa that would be always his). What had happened to change all that so quickly in Mum and Dad's eyes?

Sex: it's that obvious.

The thought that Dean would be whisking their little girl off to have his wicked way with her in Dublin, that's what changed their opinion of him. That's what had made Dean go from Golden Boy to Arch Villain in one swift move. The spectre of (potential) sex has cast a shadow over me and Dean and spoilt everything between us. That's the way my parents see it anyway. And maybe I do too. It's like there's been this tension between us all summer, knowing that Dublin is there, *looming*. . .

Wait a minute: that's not true – it's not just about the sex thing. Me and Dean: our current situation (or lack of it) isn't anything to do with whether we sleep together or not. This is about Dean: *Dean* is the one who's messed it all up. After all, it wasn't *me* who was cuddling up on a bench to a girl with a certificate in Lifesaving and Nicking Other People's Boyfriends. It wasn't *me* who was drooling over the boobs on display. Since he started work at the lido, Dean has spent more time with *her* than he has with me. And if he wasn't working alongside her or going for drinks after work with her, then he was bloody *talking* about her all the time.

OK, so I can hardly complain, seeing as I am officially on a date now. Sort of. But Dean drove

171

me to it. It's like Shaunna said that day at the lido (the day of my belly-flopping near-drowning shame); you can fancy people, but you don't have to do anything about it. So, *yes*, I had thought Marcus was cute on the three times I'd run into him at the hospital, but I wouldn't have unfurled that crumpled green paper ball from the bottom of my bag and called him, if Dean hadn't forced me into it.

"What do you fancy?" asks Marcus, passing the plastic-coated menu to me.

You, you, you. . . I think, feeling my face flush as our fingers brush. I try to smother a smirk, thinking how much Shaunna and Jude would cheer me on if they were tapped into my head and listening to that risqué joke.

"What are you smiling at?" Marcus smiles broadly himself, his teeth miraculously white and perfect against his smooth, strokeable dark skin.

"Nothing," I laugh self-consciously.

Or *would* they cheer, those best mates of mine? Once I'd forgiven Shaunna (and seen the funny side – ish) of her joke text, I'd phoned her back last night and told her everything. Annoyingly, she'd sympathized, but she hadn't seemed that convinced about Dean's guilt when it came to

Stevie. And Jude – who called me five minutes after I came off the phone to Shaunna – didn't exactly whoop with joy when I told her about my hot date today.

"What about Dean?" she'd asked.

"What *about* Dean?"

Hadn't she understood what I'd just *said*?

"But didn't he come after you? Maybe try and explain, or apologize or something?"

"I sent him a text at the pub," I told her. "I said I'd felt sick, I'd gone home, not to worry, and not to call, 'cause of Mum and Dad."

That had put a stop to him getting in touch and giving me any lame excuses about the flirting I'd spotted, sure as if I'd slapped a brick wall up between us.

As for Shaunna and Jude, well, it might be weird for them, but they were going to *have* to get used to the idea that me and Dean were finished. And they might have to get used to the idea of Marcus, if things worked out. (Fingers crossed.)

"Um . . . I think I'll have the veggie burger," I decide, running my finger over the menu and thinking that although it's my favourite, the spaghetti bolognese is too risky to try and eat on a first date. Tomato sauce dribbling down your chin is *so* not a good look. Specially for someone with such immaculate supermodel looks as me. *Not. . .*

"Yeah, I think I'll have the veggie burger too. And Coke?" he asks, then waves the waitress over as soon as he sees me nod.

With his hand raised, the short sleeve of his T-shirt slides up slightly and there's the tattoo again . . . the tiny, jet-black heart at the top of his arm.

"What?" he asks, spinning around and catching me staring.

"What?" I repeat, with a guilty jump.

And what's with the jumping? I should try to calm down – after all, we talked for ages last night, me and Marcus. I found out he's about to start studying electrical engineering at college; that the hospital orderly job is just for the summer; that he lives with his dad (Mum remarried) and has a step-brother the same age as Mia. He knows that Mia is fine, that I haven't a clue what I want to do when I leave school, and that Mum's booked me an appointment at a proper hairdresser's for the end of the week (once the scabs have healed) to have my stripes removed. I should take a deep breath and try not to be so nervous. Maybe we're not lifelong buddies, but this shouldn't be horribly awkward; it's not like it's some blind date where we've never set eyes on each other and don't have the first clue what we've got in common.

"Is it my heart?" he asks me straight out, yanking up his sleeve, all the better for me to study his tattoo.

"Um, yeah. . ." I shrug, feigning only mild interest. "It's cute."

"Cute?" he smiles, wryly.

(Uh-oh, forgot – boys don't like the word "cute". Specially if it's being used to describe something about them.)

"So. . ." I hesitate, wondering how to phrase the next, inevitably nosey question. "What made you get it done?"

"A girl," he replies frankly, running his finger around the tattoo's outline.

Oh, now *this* is interesting. Suddenly I don't feel too shy any more.

"What was her name?" I ask.

"Natalie," he smiles softly.

"How long did you go out with her?"

"Six months."

"When did you break up with her?"

"About a month ago."

"Why?"

"No real reason. It just faded out. . ."

"Unlike the tattoo?" I tease him.

"Yeah," he laughs, peering at the dark heart. "Just as well I didn't get her name done too, isn't it."

"And why didn't you?"

"Pain . . . sheer unadulterated pain! I nearly passed out getting *this* much done!"

And we're both laughing, like we're old friends with nothing to hide and nothing to feel shy about. Until Marcus hits me with a question in return.

"And you? Have you been out with anyone lately?"

I don't know what to say – my mouth opens and closes almost straight away. How do I tell him that I had a boyfriend up until ten minutes before I called him last night? That my ex-boyfriend doesn't even know he's officially "ex" yet? So I swivel my gaze out of the window and into the park, as my mind thrashes around for something to say about Dean that is truthful without being the whole, raw truth.

But staring out the window makes me less able to talk coherently than ever. If ever Fate wanted to point something out to me, it couldn't have done it better, not even if it'd arranged a giant billboard saying *Dean and Molly: over. It's official!* right outside the café window.

"Molly?" a faraway voice asks, even though Marcus is only as far away as the other side of the table.

I can't speak. I can only watch, mesmerized and shocked. Shocked at how totally gutted I feel.

"What is it?" I vaguely hear. "Is it that couple?"

I knew it was over, but I didn't know how much it would hurt to see that I was right.

"Uh-huh," I mumble, unable to tear my eyes away from Dean and Stevie, who are strolling through the park, deep in conversation, looking deep into each other's eyes.

I know it's them, even if my eyes are filling up so fast that my vision's getting cloudy.

"Someone you used to go out with?"

"Until about ten seconds ago," I blurt out, ruining my chances with Marcus for good.

"Oh."

Poor Marcus, it must be less than flattering to have your date start sobbing over her boyfriend in front of you.

"Here," he mumbles. "Have one of these. . ."

It's a tissue. OK, it's a scratchy serviette, but it'll do to mop up the mini-waterfalls that are currently coursing down my cheeks.

"Do you want to talk about it?"

I shake my head – I can't talk at all right now. There's an agonizing boulder in my throat that's making it almost impossible for me to breathe, never mind talk.

"Will I cancel the food?"

I nod.

By the time he's gone over to catch the waitress and come back, Dean and Stevie have vanished from view.

"Do you want me to walk you home?" Marcus suggests, hovering behind his chair on the other side of the table.

"No," I whisper, smiling an apologetic, wobbly smile at him. "I'll be OK."

"I'll just go then, will I? Unless you want me to stay. . ."

I shake my head. Poor Marcus; he's a nice lad who doesn't deserve to spend his day off comforting a girl who's dribbling tears on to the tablecloth over another guy.

"If you're sure you're OK. . ."

"I'm OK," I nod, still unable to control the blubbing.

"Well, bye, then."

"Bye."

And that's it. With a sad and sorry wave from

him, and an equally sad and sorry wave in return from me, Marcus ambles out of the café and out of my life.

Do you think I could win a prize for the shortest date in the history of the world. . .?

chapter seventeen

Life is a roller coaster...

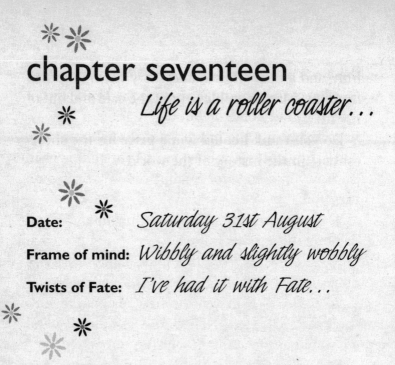

Date: *Saturday 31st August*

Frame of mind: *Wibbly and slightly wobbly*

Twists of Fate: *I've had it with Fate...*

Definitions of fun:

1) Piling on a train with Jude, Shaunna and a few ridiculously heavy bags that make us look like we've packed for a fortnight in Crete instead of the seaside for a long weekend.

2) Squealing at each other as we tear around the caravan and play with all the pull-out, button-pressing, space-saving gadgets. (One drawback:

the loo is of minuscule, knee-bashing proportions. Our kneecaps are going to be one big bruise by the time we head home on Sunday night.)

3) Exploring the beach (and the talent on it), and eating chips, ice-cream and more chips from the rows and rows of quaint, old-style cafés on the prom.

4) Stumbling on a brilliant club in town and dancing till our feet hurt.

5) Giggling our way back to the caravan park in our bare feet at midnight, eating yet *more* chips.

So that was Friday – the first of our precious three days used up. Now here was Saturday and we were busy keeping up our fun quota.

Well, we *were*, up until twenty minutes ago when I ruined everything. . .

"Drink that," Shaunna orders me, sploshing a steaming mug down on the formica table.

"What is it?" I ask, sniffing gingerly.

"Hot water."

Shaunna folds her arms across her chest and looks at me defiantly, daring me to complain.

"But we're on holiday!" I complain anyway. "There's no one around to check up on us! Can't I have something more exciting than hot water?"

"It'll settle your stomach."

That's Jude, backing Shaunna up, as she

stretches her long, skinny bare legs along the length of the caravan's padded banquette, and nibbles on a handful of M&Ms she's just helped herself to from the family-size bag on the table.

Outside, the midday sun is streaming down, hot and blisteringly bright. But because of me, my friends are stuck in a stuffy caravan right now, administering kindness and cups of H_2O, bless 'em.

"Yeah – that's the last time we let *you* go on a roller coaster!" Shaunna waggles a finger in my face.

Ah, the roller coaster . . . it wasn't *just* the stomach-heaving twists and dips of the Wildcat ride that was responsible for me losing my breakfast over the pier edge. It was all sorts of stuff, starting with that breakfast itself (deep-fried everything). Of course, the sickly-sweet Happy Hour cocktails I'd tried last night probably didn't help either. And then there was the knot of guilt that kept tightening in my stomach every time I thought about Dean, and what I'd done. . .

"This isn't about Dean, again, is it?"

"Dean?! No way, Shaun!" I say in surprise, gripping my steaming mug of hot water (mmm . . . delicious) just hard enough and long enough to burn my hand. "What makes you say that?"

"Let's see. . ." sighs Shaunna, hitching up her sarong and settling herself down at the other end of the long banquette from Jude.

"You wrote his name in the sand with your toes this morning," Jude butts in, leaning an arm behind her head and gazing lazily at me. "Didn't she, Shaun?"

"Yep, and then you doodled his name on the serviette at the café we had breakfast in."

Did I?

"And you're doing it again right now. . ." Jude points out, leaning forward and indicating the letters I've been unconsciously spelling out in the spilt sugar on the table.

"That's three times, Mol, so I guess that proves *something*."

"Three's a charm. . ." I hear myself mumble in response to Shaunna.

"A charm for what?" she fires straight back. "Do you want to get back together with Dean?"

"No!" I snap in surprise. "It's just . . . it's just that I wish I hadn't finished with him the way I did."

And I wished he hadn't kept phoning and leaving messages on my mobile all week, even though I'd specifically asked him not to.

"So you chucked him by letter," Shaunna

shrugs. "So what? He's not the *first* person to find out he's been dumped that way. What *matters* is that you feel dumping him was the right thing to do."

"It was! It is! He's seeing someone else – right?"

Why do I get the feeling they're both still on Dean's side?

"Right, fine," Shaunna holds her hands up, as if she's putting an end to any more arguing on the subject.

Jude, meanwhile, brushes the stray sugar crystals off the table and into her hand, then drops them into the pedal bin, with a resounding thunk of the lid. So that's the subject of Dean dealt with, then.

Both of my friends stay so silent, that the sip of hot water I force myself to take sounds like it's wired up to an amplifier.

I feel like they're expecting me to say something, so I say it.

"Look, I saw something, OK?"

"Saw what?" asks Shaunna, her puzzled frown matching Jude's.

"When we came off the Wildcat – I saw something, and it upset me."

There, I've started to tell them: there's no going back now. I'm about to enter a conversation where

Shaunna will tell me I'm overreacting, Jude will agree, and I'll look like a dumb, hyper-emotional geek – yet again. But my whole stupid summer's been like this, so why stop now?

"Well, what was it you saw?"

Shaunna's face is full of concern. Oh God, I've made it sound like I saw a flasher, or someone chucking a body-shaped binbag off the pier or something.

"It was when we came off the Wildcat," I explain hurriedly. "I. . . I saw a fortune telling booth. It was *her*. You know, that fortune-teller woman who gave me the terrible reading."

"The woman in the beige cardie?" Jude checks, as Shaunna's shoulders sag and she lets out a sigh of relief and irritation all in one.

"Yes, her. Don't you think that's weird?" I hurry to justify myself. "The way I keep seeing her everywhere? It's like she's haunting me!"

"For God's sake, Molly, she's not dead!" Shaunna laughs out loud. "She's a fortune-teller! She travels around the area, setting up wherever she can get work! It's her job – even if she isn't very good at it!"

"I know *that*! I guess that's what suddenly made me feel so bad. All that stuff I believed at the beginning of summer – the way I thought I could figure out what Fate was trying to tell me through all those coincidences: that was all rubbish! And seeing that woman again just reminded me what a mess I made of everything. . ."

I actually think I went into shock after I saw Mrs BC; the shock of realizing that I'd managed to ruin my own summer because I was trying so hard *not* to! OK, so being sick was a bit of an extreme reaction I know, but running to the edge of the pier and barfing into the blue waves below was a kind of release.

Everything hideous and horrible tumbled away: endless mud-logged fields; creepy Cameron and his suction snog; getting sacked from my job; guilt over Mia and the goat-bite; guilt over fancying Marcus; guilt about mucking Marcus around; the shame of nearly drowning 'cause I was too busy being jealous of Stevie to look what I was doing; the shame of being *rescued* by Stevie; the Bagpuss stripes and burnt head; the fall-outs I'd had with my parents; the fall-outs I'd had with my friends over this holiday and Dean; my growing irritation with Dean; the twist of the knife seeing Stevie and Dean together last weekend. . .

"Look Shaunna – she's at it again!" Jude exclaims.

"Molly!"

 186

My eyes dart from Jude and Shaunna's faces to the table, which they're both staring down at.

Wow.

Without even knowing I was doing it, I've just spelt out Dean's name in M&Ms.

"I don't know what's wrong with me. . ." I sigh, putting my head in my hands. "I think I'm going *mad*."

Once upon a time, I was the sensible one out of the three of us. Now, if anyone was to describe us, they'd say, "Shaunna's the funny one, Jude's a bit scatty, and Molly? Molly's just *mental*."

"You want to know what we think?" I hear Shaunna say.

Uh-oh – she said "we". I have obviously been discussed. I don't suppose I'm going to like what she's about to tell me. . .

"No, but go on," I reply, tilting my head up but staring at them both through the gaps in my fingers.

"You still love Dean."

"No, I don't. Not any more," I shake my hidden head. "Is that it?"

"Yes you do love Dean, and no, that's not 'it'. The thing is, me and Jude know *exactly* when you started to go weird and grouchy."

"And mad," adds Jude, very helpfully.

187

I blink questioningly at my friends, feeling my eyelashes brush against my fingers.

"It was when Dean asked you to go on holiday with him."

"That's not exactly true, Shaunna. . ."

I let my fingers fall from my burning-with-embarrassment face as I speak. (Chemicals . . . embarrassment . . . my skin was definitely taking a bashing this week, just like my pride is right now.) But I can't quite bring myself to look my friends in the eye.

"Bet you it *is* true."

"It's not!" I insist.

"'Tis!"

"Not!"

"'Tis!"

"Not!"

"'Tis not!"

"'Tis!"

"Aha! Gotcha!" giggles Shaunna, her index finger aimed right at me.

Damn! She got me with that stupid kid trick!

"OK," I eyeball the girls. "So *why* do you think I went weird about the holiday?"

"Well. . ."

Shaunna flips Jude a look, before she turns back to me.

 188

"It freaked you out, didn't it? The whole idea of sleeping with him?"

Wow – could she *be* more blunt? Or right.

"It wasn't just the holiday," I hear myself mumble. "It started way back – when we were doing our exams. There was this one night when we— well, we nearly. . . And since then it's been OK – I mean, we haven't ever. . ."

I'm struggling here. And not just 'cause it's really hard to say that sort of stuff out loud. It's mainly because something has become really obvious to me all of a sudden. Poor Dean . . . he'd been running round organizing the whole Ireland trip, while I'd been putting the brakes on in my head, trying *anything* to get out of it, including falling out with him. But the bottom line is, I wasn't ready for it. I wasn't ready for it that night we babysat, and even now – months later – it's still not right. To be honest, I was really, deep-down *glad* when Mum and Dad came down like a tonne of bricks on the whole idea and said no way to us going on holiday together. . .

"But you thought when you were in Ireland, it *would* happen?"

I nod at Jude.

"And you're right – it did freak me out."

"I don't suppose you ever—"

"No, Shaunna – I never spoke to Dean about any of this."

She doesn't tell me off, I'm glad to see. I feel stupid enough as it is. Back in the days when I was The Sensible One, if Shaunna and Adam had been going through the same situation, I'd have been the first person doling out the advice about how important it is to be honest with each other. And now, all I've done is drive the best thing that's ever happened to me into the arms of Stevie, who's *bound* to want to give Dean more than the kiss of life. . .

"Don't feel bad, just 'cause you didn't feel right about going the whole way with Dean yet. After all, it *is* a big thing!"

Shaunna started that sentence sensitively, then cracks up immediately when she realizes how her best Agony Aunt wording *actually* came out.

And that's us all off . . . sniggering like juvenile ten year olds who have just heard a bum joke.

Me, Shaunna and Jude – it's taken sex, puke and a bad taste innuendo, but I haven't felt this close to the two of them in *ages*. And it's great.

"So, Mental Molly; have you definitely given up on your coincidence theory?" Shaunna changes the subject, as soon as we start getting our breath back.

"Yep," I nod, wiping the tears of laughter from my eyes. "That's all a load of pants. So you can just drop the 'Mental' thing, please."

"Oh, yeah?" Shaunna beams. "Well, what do you call *that*, then?"

I spin round and look out the window. And there he is, bumbling around between the caravans, looking lost and bewildered.

"Oi, Big Boy!" Shaunna jumps up and yells from the open doorway, glancing back and giving me and Jude a knowing wink. "We're over here!"

Dean beams one of his gorgeous, nose-crinkling smiles and my heart does a backward flip. . .

chapter eighteen

Chips, cake and one last coincidence...

Date: *Sunday 8th September*

Frame of mind: *Fluffy*

Twists of Fate: *A sprinkle of rain and a favour for a friend?*

"Dean!" I yell, finally shooing him off me and wiping the slobber from my face. "What was *that* all about?"

"It was just a birthday kiss!" he grins wickedly. "In the style of your old flame, Cameron! *Ooof!* Well, that's how you *like* to be kissed, isn't it? Come on you – *ooow!* – know you love it!"

I love Dean, but I don't know if I love being teased about someone I'd rather forget. I think Dean's getting the message, since I'm thumping him with the giant white rabbit he's just given me. (Don't panic – it's a toy.)

"Hey, you two! Hurry up!" Adam's voice yells from the open French doors. "Your mum's got the surprise birthday cake ready, Molly! Oh . . . sorry, Mrs Palmer. . ."

"Can I have a proper kiss before we go inside?" Dean murmurs, leaning close and wrapping his arms around me and the fat bunny.

"Yes, you most certainly can," I smile, before our lips meld together.

Wow. . .

Wow to the kiss; wow to being more in love than I've ever been; wow to what a difference two weeks can make. Life is good: there are no black clouds hovering over my head (apart from the one that's started sprinkling rain on this otherwise sunshiny afternoon, sending everyone else at my birthday barbecue scurrying inside). And my parents don't hate Dean any more (after I sat them down and had a long, *very* embarrassing chat with them, assuring them both that me and Dean weren't planning on doing . . . well, "*it*" any time soon).

And me and Dean? Well, Dean turning up at the caravan park that Saturday afternoon – it didn't make me start believing in the cosmic power of coincidences again.

OK, it *did* for about a minute, till Shaunna and Jude confessed that it was a big set-up. After a week of going loopy when I blanked his calls, Dean had done the only thing he could think of; he begged my best mates for help. Shaunna and Jude felt sorry for him (and me), and arranged for Dean and Adam to drive three long hours to the seaside, all so that me and Dean could spend time talking, explaining, and remembering why we were so good together in the first place.

And it worked. By the time Shaunna, Adam and Jude arrived back – with chips – we'd sorted it all out. Dean had told me all about Stevie, about how she'd done a Cameron and turned psycho on him. She'd lulled Dean into a false sense of security by acting all matey (he was too dumb to spot when it flipped to blatant flirting), then pounced on him when he least expected, i.e. the day I saw him in the park, when she asked him if he fancied a stroll during their lunch-hour. A stroll, yeah; a big snog-up, no thank you. He said she'd nearly fallen in the fountain, he'd pushed her away so hard in surprise.

 194

Of course, I ended up blurting out what happened with creepy Cameron, and then there seemed no point in secrets since we were having this big truth session, so I splurged it all out about my three-minute date with Marcus. Dean was hurt, I could tell, but he put a brave face on and tried to pretend it didn't matter.

Then came the uncomfortable truth about Dublin – and that night back at the beginning of summer – and how I really felt about . . . *everything*. Dean just took one look at my flushed-with-shyness face and hugged me so tight to his chest that I could hardly hear him telling me I was a doughball and stupid for not saying anything and that he loved me to pieces and that we could take things as slow as I liked. . .

So here we are in my garden, getting speckled with rain, and not caring one tiny bit. If I wasn't busy kissing my boyfriend (of exactly one year and eight days), I'd probably be spinning around on the grass, my arms outstretched and grinning with happiness. . .

"Molly, leave that poor boy alone!" Shaunna shouts from the French doors.

"Yeah – stop trying to make those of us without boyfriends jealous!" Jude adds.

195

"Better go in!" I grin at Dean, as we step apart and turn towards the house.

"Yeah, I guess we'd better – you've still got to thank your gran for your necklace!"

He's nodding at the heart-shaped locket around my neck.

(Yes, it's from Argos; no, my forgetful gran has no idea she gave me the exact same present five years ago; and yes, she did write *"Happy Birthday, Mia!"* on my card. . .)

Shaunna and Jude are waving at us to hurry up, while Adam appears back in the doorway with a shrieking Mia on his shoulders.

"Pity Jude can't find someone nice," I mutter, squeezing Dean's hand as I watch Shaunna turn and laugh fondly at her goofball of a boyfriend.

"She'll find someone. She deserves to meet a nice guy."

And suddenly, I sense a shiver; as if a finger has run up and down my back. What about Marcus? *He's* a nice guy . . . Jude would love him – if I sell him to her right. Maybe it wasn't a coincidence that I met him; maybe it was meant to be, like when I met Dean through Shaunna. I've still got that green paper towel with his number on it somewhere. Maybe. . .

"So, do you really like your present?" asks Dean, disturbing my train of thought.

"Yes, I love it," I nod, hugging the white ball of fluff close, as we walk up to the house.

"At least it's better than the *last* thing I bought you. At least *this* won't stain you green."

"True."

Yes, I've told him about the ring I can't wear. Hey, it's 100% honesty all the way with us now. . .

"Do you like the stripes?"

I fluff up the bunny's customized ginger highlights (painted on courtesy of Shaunna – who else?)

"The stripes are the best thing about it!" I tell him confidently, since two expensive trips to the hairdresser have now more-or-less transformed my own hair back to its normal milky colour. Thank God.

"So, got a birthday wish for when you blow out the candles, Mol?"

"Yeah," I nod at Dean. "I wish that no one dares say 'Snap!' when they see me and this rabbit together..."

But the best present of all is feeling like I've got my life (and my head) back to normal – thanks to being back with Dean, this time with no stupid secrets and pointless jealousy and cosmic weirdness getting in our way.

Except that now I think of it, Mrs Beige

Cardie . . . didn't she say I'd find true love by the end of the summer? And isn't she right, in a way?

Well, whether her fortune-telling was phoney or fluke, who cares: Happy, blissed-out Birthday to me. . .

Want to know more about Shaunna,
Jude and Molly?

Then don't miss:

my Funny Valentine

"Aaaaaaaaaaaaaaaaaiiiiiiiiiiiiiiiiiiiiiiiiiieeeeeeeeeeeeeeee!"

That, if you want to know, is my mother. Don't worry – she is not being murdered.

"Eeeeeeeeeeeeiiiiiiiiiiiiiiiiiiiiiiiaaaaaaaaaaaaaaaa!"

And that is my big sister Ruth. She's twenty. She is *also* not being murdered.

They are the only two people in the room screaming. My dad isn't screaming, but he is making this odd, surprised-sounding *"Harrumph!"* noise and is self-consciously trying to hug Boring Brian (my sister's boyfriend). Only Dad chickens out halfway into the hug, and turns it into a few manly pats on the back instead. Boring Brian is blushing and smiling and trying not to crumple under my dad's over-enthusiastic patting.

Ah, but I've got something wrong here – Boring Brian is *not* Ruth's boyfriend. As of now, he is officially her *fiancé*. This is what they've just announced, and this is what all the screaming and back-thumping is about.

"Isn't that lovely, Shaunna? Your sister's *engaged*!"

Mum turns a little too quickly and catches me looking blank-faced. (Lucky she didn't catch me half-a-second earlier when I was wincing from the pain of her and Ruth's high-pitched howling.)

In a panic, I stick on a smile and nod back, hoping I'm coming across enthusiastic enough.

"Mmm!" I manage to mumble non-committally.

It's not that I'm cynical or hard-hearted or anything – *honestly* I'm not. I'm really pleased for Ruth, if that's what she wants. It's just that it's all so . . . *predictable*.

"Oh, Ruth, on Valentine's Day too!" Mum gushes at my sister, letting me relax my fake smile slightly. "It's *such* a surprise! And *so* romantic!"

Now there's my point – that last bit of what my mum's said? It's *so* not true. It is *so* not a surprise that Ruth and Boring Brian are engaged. I mean, they've been going out together since . . . well, practically since the dawn of time, and they've always made it totally clear that their life plan was to get engaged/married/have 2.4 children/an estate car and a Tesco Club Card, and anything else would be a big let-down. I'd have been more surprised if they'd announced that they weren't *ever* going to get engaged, or that they were splitting up. But this? This is about as surprising as the Ten o'clock News having depressing bits in it, or being told that cats go miaow and dogs go woof.

And as for romantic? They got engaged on *Valentine's* Day. I'm sorry, but that's not romantic – that's just *corny*.

"Oh, Mum, it was so fantastic!" Ruth is saying, clutching Mum's hands. "Brian took me to Franco's tonight –"

Now you see; that proves my point again. Franco's is this glorified takeaway pizza place that's been running ads all week in the local paper saying, "*Hey fellas – why not treat that special lady to a two-for-the-price-of-one pizza deal for Valentine's Day?*" Why not? I'll tell you why not – because it's naff, *that's* why not. Specially when the ad goes on to promise "*a candle on every table!*", like that's some big wow. It's just that if Boring Brian *had* to propose on Valentine's Day (pass me the sick-bucket, please), why couldn't he do something like . . . I dunno, like . . . ask Ruth to marry him down at the beach at midnight, under the moon and stars, with the dark sea crashing spectacularly in the background. . . Not in sodding two-for-the-price-of-one Franco's, along with every other sucker who thinks a candle rammed in a bottle and some cheesy taped Italian music playing in the background is the height of romance.

"– and then this man came round the tables selling flowers," Ruth is gushing, "and Brian bought me a single red rose –"

Arrgghhhh! Not a single red rose, Brian! You could have surprised her with a bunch of beautiful tulips; an armful of arum lilies; a fistful of freesias; a bundle of buttercups. . . Ten-out-of-ten for choosing the *least* original flower in the world!

"– and then Brian went down on one knee and said to me, 'Ruth –'"

Oh, no – Mum's got her hand to her mouth, like she can't believe what's coming next.

"– he said, 'Ruth . . . will you marry me?'!"

Why is Mum gasping? Brian wasn't exactly going to get down on his knees and say, "Ruth – I'm a transvestite, and I'm leaving tomorrow to work on a cruise liner as a Jane McDonald tribute act!" (Although it would have been a lot more interesting if he had. . .)

Now Mum and Ruth are hugging, and – I'm pretty sure – crying, while Dad and Brian beam at them and each other and silently nod a lot. Me? I'm not sure what to do. I know I should be joining in the girlie hug-fest, but I'd feel like a big, fat fake. So, I just stand, like one of the boys, beaming and nodding.

"And you know the best thing, Mum?" Ruth sniffles happily, and shoots a watery-eyed look at her proud fiancé.

"What's that, sweetie?" asks Mum, ferreting out a paper tissue from somewhere up her sleeve and dabbing at her eyes.

"We've decided to get married. . ."

My sister pauses for dramatic effect, but my heart's already sinking, 'cause I just *know* what she's going to say.

". . .*next* Valentine's Day!" Ruth squeals.

"*Aaaaaaaaaaaaaaaiiiiiiiiiiiiiiiiiiiiiieeeeeeeeeeeeee-eeeeee!*"

Urgh – Mum's off again.

"I know! *Eeeeeeeeeiiiiiiiiiiiiiiiiiiiiiiaaaaaaaaaaaa-aaaaaa!*"

And they're both back doing the hugging and

crying thing, and if I don't escape in two seconds flat I won't have any eardrums left.

"Listen! I'm going to nip across to Jude's and tell her the news!" I say, coming out with the perfect response to get me out of there and still look like I'm impressed by the whole not-very-surprising surprise announcement.

"OK, love," Mum nods distractedly in my direction, too excited to look at her watch and comment that it's nearly ten o'clock and a bit late on a school night to go disturbing the Conrads.

Ruth gives me the sweetest, wibbly-wobbly little smile and wiggles her fingers at me. She's lovely, my sister, even if she does settle for ordinary.

"And remember, Shaunna!" Ruth blinks at me, all dewy-eyed. "There's only *one* person I want as my bridesmaid!"

I'm kind of hoping she's talking about Justine or Penny or one of her other mates when she says that, but I have this funny feeling (called dread) that it's *me* she wants to see in a flouncy frock. . .

As it happens, Mum is wrong: "the Conrads" are only too glad to be disturbed. At least the one who's at home is. Jude flings open the door to me and says, "Thank God! A human!" and ushers me in.

See, my mum doesn't *get* that other people don't live exactly the same as us. You know; two, smiley parents who stay home in the evenings watching *Casualty* and *The Weakest Link*, two nice daughters who work hard (me at school doing GSCEs; Ruth at college studying Hotel Management), in our nice, cosy house. Jude's set-up is slightly different – maybe she lives in a practically identical house across the street, but, in *her* living room, there's no mum tut-tutting at Anne Robinson's rudeness. After being dumped by Jude's dad a few years back, her mum spent six months in a pit of gloom, then rose phoenix-like to take on the world – which involved ditching the "Mrs" tag and getting everyone (including Jude) to call her by her first name (Helen); studying for a degree; getting a whole new bunch of (much younger) friends from university; and basically managing somehow – in the midst of all the hard studying and hard partying – to forget the fact that she's got a fifteen-year-old daughter she's meant to be looking after.

"Where's Helen tonight?" I ask, following Jude through the hall.

"Who knows?" shrugs Jude, reaching for a big cardie that's draped over the end of the banister. "She's on this planning committee for some rally or something about student loans. They're supposed to be organizing it tonight, which probably means they're all in a *pub* somewhere."

Ooh, that came out a bit bitter. That's the trouble; *I* think Jude's mum is pretty inspirational (Helen's been planning a rally this evening while *my* mum's been planning tomorrow night's *tea*), but I know it's tough on Jude. It's hard to get your head around the fact that your mum is having a better social life than you.

"Um, where are we going?" I ask, as Jude hauls on the duvet-sized cardie and heads for the back door.

"Got to have a smoke," she replies, waving a cigarette at me. "I'm having a crisis."

Me and Molly hate the fact that Jude smokes. So does her mum, which is why we are now going to perch ourselves on the bench at the bottom of the garden in the freezing cold, so that no tell-tale fumes can slither anywhere near the house, and give her away. Luckily, Jude only ever smokes when she's having a crisis. Unluckily, she tends to have about thirty crises a week.

"What's up?" I frown, pulling the sleeves of my jumper down over my hands as I stomp after her down the path.

"Got that thingy test tomorrow and I haven't

studied for it," she says, flopping on to the flaky wooden bench that faces away from the garden and house and into the dark leafiness of Westburn Park, just beyond the high, metal-railed fence.

"Why haven't you studied for it?" I ask Jude, sitting myself next to her and hugging my knees up to my chin.

"Dunno. I tried to . . . but I got distracted, and then . . . just didn't get round to it."

Loads of people would love to live in a house free of nagging parents – like me, even if mine are the kind that try and *coax* you along rather than the kind who threaten to kneecap you if you don't tidy your knicker drawer or whatever. But Jude, she's the sort of girl that *needs* someone nagging her – nicely or not – or she never gets anything done. And Helen's got this optimistic view that Jude's grown-up enough and responsible enough to sort her own life out. Ha – fat chance.

"Anyway, distract me," Jude pleads. "I don't want to think about tests and . . . and. . ."

She's wafting her horrible, smelly cigarette in the air while she thinks what she's trying to say.

"*Not* having swotted for tests?" I suggest helpfully.

"Yeah, *that*," she grumbles bleakly. "So, go on – what's brought you skipping over here?"

And so I tell her about Ruth and Boring Brian, and their cheesy engagement in cheesy old Franco's. And Jude goes all melty on me.

"Don't you see what I mean, though?" I say, slightly exasperated and flapping her smoke away. "It's just that I *know* it's nice for Ruth and everything, but don't you think it's just all too corny?"

"Shaunna, it's *never* going to happen like *you* want it," Jude grins at me, which exasperates me even more. "You think love's all about some *special* boy coming along and *whisking* you off to New Mexico on the back of his motorbike, where you'll sit beside a campfire in the desert, listening to him strumming his guitar and playing a song he's written *specially* for you, and every morning you'll wake up with a cactus rose placed on your pillow that he's plucked for you at dawn. . ."

"OK! OK! Quit it!" I stop her, hating hearing her trash one of my favourite fantasies.

What gets me is that all the girls I know – including Jude and Molly – they go out with these lads who seem to communicate in the language of Grunt. They think "special" is if a boy phones when he says he will. I don't want to sound pushy here, but there've got to be boys out there with more soul, more imagination than that. Haven't there? So, yeah, I *do* day-dream about being whisked off into the heat and dust of New Mexico by someone amazing. I *do* yearn for a boy who'd want to write a song for me, or paint my portrait, or name a star after me. But it's not like I live on Planet Airhead and think that stuff is the only way someone can prove they're special. I'd settle for a lad that would send me a card, just saying something stupid like, "Hi, Shaunna – happy Thursday!" Or a boy who'd drape daisy chains around my neck. Or a guy who wanted to make snow angels in the park in the middle of winter. . .

"You've got to get real, Shaunna," Jude gently nags at me in a school-teacher tone, "or you'll *never* get a boyfriend."

Now that really, *really* bugs me. OK, so I'm fifteen and have never had a boyfriend. And while that hacks me off sometimes, at least I'm not like Jude, who's been out with loads of losers and had her heart broken by every single, last, loser one of them. If she can't even see the irony in that, then I'm not going to try and explain it to her. In fact, I'm so mad, I can't even answer her, so I just stare off into the park – where I can hear the distant cackle of laughter – and ignore her.

In the daytime, the park is really pretty, in a standard trees/flowers/fountain/bandstand kind of way. But I kind of like it more now, all dark and Gothic, with its few curlicued Victorian street-lamps dotted around the paths, casting a weird mustardy glow over everything. All the neighbours whose houses back on to the park – like Jude's – they're always writing into the local paper to moan about the gangs of juvenile thugs/ assorted weirdos/potential burglars they're convinced sneak in there and loiter with intent once the park is locked up.

Me and Jude think they're just a right a load of spoilsports – the old fogey neighbours, I mean. It's only ever kids mucking about, and that's only 'cause there's not much to do round here at nights, specially in winter. In fact, I can hear more of the distant laughter now – and it just sounds like a bunch of lads, not rampaging hooligans or anything. It's not like there's every any real troub—

Omigod . . . under the lamppost nearest Jude's house. . .

[My stomach's just lurched in the weirdest way.]

It's a boy . . . maybe about seventeen . . . he's stopped . . . he's gazing up at the sky. . .

[*What's he looking at?* I wonder, raising my eyes to the clear, velvety sky and its sprinkling of stars. Nice . . . but not as interesting as this boy, who I'm staring at again now.]

His face is bathed in light from the lamp. . .

[Yikes – my heart rate has surged from 0 to 150 in five seconds. What's going on?]

His dark hair is flopping back to show off sharp cheekbones . . . sort of Slavic eyes. . . He is. . .

[My heart's beating so fast I'm getting *breathless*.]

He is. . .

[I never believed in lust at first sight before.]

He is . . . absolutely *beautiful*. . .

"I know *I'd* love it if someone wanted to buy *me* a red rose," Jude suddenly starts mumbling, "never mind ask me to *marry* them."

[The spell the boy's cast over me is broken, and instantly my heart rate calms down slightly – mainly because I've remembered to take a breath again, after unconsciously holding it for the last 60 seconds.]

"Shhh!" I hiss at Jude, grabbing her by the arm and pointing over to the boy standing under the lamp.

He's still there, alone, blinking up at the stars and the moon. . .

"Looks a bit dodgy to me," Jude frowns, leaning forward and screwing up her eyes for a better look.

"He's not dodgy – he's *gorgeous*!" I whisper,

watching him move away from the pool of light under the lamp and head for the silhouetted band-stand.

"If he's not dodgy, then what's he doing hanging around on his own like that for?" Jude whispers back.

"I don't know! Let's just watch him!" I tell her in my teeny-tiniest voice.

As my eyes adjust to the darkness, I can make out his shape – long and lean – sitting down on the steps of the bandstand, where he reaches down and pulls out . . . I don't know what, exactly.

"What the hell is *that*!" squeaks Jude.

"It's . . . it's. . ." I say frantically, straining my eyes and hoping this vision of beautiful boy-ness isn't going to turn out to be a park pervert after all.

"Whatever it is, it's huge!" Jude sniggers.

"Look! Look! He's lifting it up! It's OK! It's a telescope!" I cry out in relief, then slap my hand over my mouth, hoping he hasn't heard me. He hasn't (phew).

Yes! He's still a vision of beautiful boy-ness, and he's a beautiful boy who is right at this moment lost in the rings of Saturn, or the swirling red dust of Mars, or the deep, unfathomable recesses of the moon. . .

As I gaze at him star-gazing, I realize I'm holding

my breath again, and Jude might be too, she's gone so quiet.

Oops – he's heard something. . . He's suddenly dropped the telescope from his eyes and is casting around sharply – stopping (gasp!) and staring for a second in our direction. Can he really see us? Aren't we lost in the darkness, tucked away from the house lights behind us and the streetlamps in front of us? Or has the pinprick of orange light from Jude's cigarette signalled to him that he's being spied on? Part of me desperately wants our drool-fest to stay secret, but part of me is frantically sending out magnetic beams from my eyes to his. . .

But in two seconds flat, it's all over; as quickly as he appeared, the boy is gone – swallowed up by a baying bunch of boys who have just swooped and thundered along the path, shouting at him that the park-keeper's coming.

"Huh! Here we go!" Jude grumbles, turning around and noticing lights flickering into life in nearby houses. "Nosy neighbours, to your windows, double-quick time, please!"

But I don't look round – I'm still trying to follow him; trying to work out which of the vanishing distant shadows is The Boy.

"Come on; let's go in – before one of the old

farts spots me with a fag and reports me to Helen. . ." Jude jokes, standing up and shivering.

"Sure," I reply, following her back up the path.

But just before I step though the back door into the brightness and warmth, I take one quick, last look into the now-silent, inky dark-green of Westburn Park.

I only saw him for a couple of minutes and I might never see him again. But somehow I feel, in the pit of my madly fluttering stomach, that I won't be forgetting that boy – that Star-Boy – in a hurry. . .

SIGN UP NOW!

For exclusive news, competitions and further information about Karen and her books, sign up to the Karen McCombie newsletter now!

Just email

publicity@scholastic.co.uk

And don't forget to check out her website –

www.karenmccombie.com

brain full of plots, stupid stuff and cat hair

KM°C

THE AUTHOR

Karen says…

"It's sheeny and shiny, furry and er, funny in places! It's everything you could want from a website and a weeny bit more…"